BREVET WEDGE

a Charlemagne File

K.A. Bachus

Cover by Marigold Faith

CHARLEMAGNE FILES TIMELINE

Short Story Collection
A Lighter Shade of Night,
mid 60s to early 70s

Novels
Trinity Icon, early 70s
Cetus Wedge, early 80s
Brevet Wedge, nine months later
Lion Tamer, five months later
State of Nature, early 90s
Vory, a year later
Swallow, five weeks later
Quiet Move, late 90s
Goat Rope, 1999

CONTENTS

A spy's worst enemy is another spy…

—John LeCarré, *The Pigeon Tunnel*

Brevet — A commission promoting a military
officer in rank without an increase in pay

PROLOGUE

He wanted to kill her.

Nick tapped the ash from the end of his cigarette into an ashtray on the bedside table. He looked at the straw-colored head lying on the pillow next to him. The blankets were none too clean, the sheets a dingy grey in the morning light, but the motel constituted pure luxury for a thief from the Soviet Gulag. He had come far, but this vile woman made the killers he had known seem like saints. They were all hot, vicious, and effective. She epitomized the cold, thoughtless, and selfish. He would rather die by the hand of the first than live with the second.

"You're not still mad at me, are you Nick?" She yawned and stretched bare arms, awakened by the intensity of his stare.

He had a glimpse of one surgically enhanced breast. "It was irresponsible," he said.

"I know. But I did it so we could be together. You'll see. We'll have the insurance money and can go anywhere we want. David will be in college and it'll be just us."

"The people you hired are dead," he told her, snubbing one cigarette and lighting another.

She reached for the one he had started, so he lit yet another for himself.

"I didn't hire anybody," she said after a long drag.

"The ones you manipulated your husband into hiring."

"Oh."

He wanted to tell her all of it, scream it into her face. He clamped his jaw shut lest he lose control.

She blew the smoke through pursed lips and turned to look at him. "Did they get the guy? Ricky's enemy, I mean. Did they get him before they died? Do you think their friends will go after Ricky now, or should I tip off the FBI to make sure?"

Her single-minded ruthlessness took his breath away. He could not explain to her that her actions would not only kill her husband, which was her desired outcome but also put him in jeopardy. He presumed it was not what she wanted, but he couldn't be certain.

"Why the Chinese?" he asked.

"My uncle…. I thought you would be proud of me."

Proud of her? Admiring of her cutthroat proclivities, her inventive, though imbecile, means of achieving her ends? And those ends were directly contrary to anything that might be good for him. He wanted to tell her about the man whose throat had been cut and also what it meant.

"I needed Ricky alive."

"But you said last night that they failed. So he is alive. You're confusing me."

"Six men are dead, Linda. The people who killed them will come for Ricky. They are smart people."

"You know who they are?"

"Yes."

"Maybe you can get them to finish the job, Nick."

It was a germ of an idea, emanating from an evil source, but if he could entice them to rid him of her as well, it would be worth it.

ONE

As a senior intelligence officer, I can't not make a record, no matter what Mack says. I will lock this up at my bank rather than at work since I now know how unsecure all secret systems are. All the caveats and classifications apply. This is WEDGE material. I'm taping it so I can truthfully say I didn't write anything down.

It began as I enjoyed a brief, rapturous moment pulling into my driveway on Friday evening before a long holiday weekend and the beginning of an entire week off.

Oh, wondrous release from the politics—and by God, my job has developed some political strains—the nagging worries, the inanities, the constant battering I receive from above and below. Goodbye, dungeon-like, windowless office. Hello doting, half-dotty, but loving wife, who holds my martini, shaken, not stirred, ready for my imbibing. Sigh.

Sharp intake of breath.

A car with two blond men in it sat parked in front of my house. It was not the usual black Mercedes, but I know Mack when I see him, and I never wanted to see the cutthroat son of a bitch at my house. He did not acknowledge me, though he was frankly watching me. So was his son.

I marched through my front door with my hand on my Walther PPK, ready to do hopeless battle against the missing Frenchman. *I'm sorry about what happened, you assholes, but my family is fucking off limits.* Dear God, I was beginning to sound like Steve and I was ready to fight like him, too, in whatever way my short, round body would allow it.

I was prepared to take the Frenchman apart. He grinned at me from the corner seat at the kitchen table with what I knew had to be my martini sitting in front of him. Steve stood at the kitchen sink drying a crystal glass for my wife Maryann, because she won't let such things go in the dishwasher. She bustled over to the refrigerator, pulled out the shaker, and poured the remains of a batch into a fresh martini glass. It was already in my hand when she added the olive. I stood quivering and my shaking hand threatened to spill the over-full drink, so I threw half of it down my throat to preserve it.

Only the Frenchman, sometimes called Louis, appreciated the state I was in. I could tell by the way he grinned at me. His black eyes twinkled with that mixture of merry madness that always made me shudder. He had grey hair mixed in the dark brown at his temples. It reminded me that the little bit I still have is even more grey. Maryann and Steve joked and jabbered away as usual, the same way they did when we had the Donovans over for barbecue on the happy day of my granddaughter's baptism.

Louis sat in the corner, leaning back and spreading his jacket open so the leather straps of his shoulder rig, the stock of his gun, and the cases of extra magazines on his belt, all advertised themselves directly to my eyes. Yes, he was saying to me, you are right to worry. But don't be stupid.

"Leo," said my wife, "Sally and little Danny are coming to stay for the weekend. Isn't that lovely?" Maryann did not know my game name was Frank Cardova. She didn't know I had a game name. She was overall ignorant of the game I was in.

Maryann thinks all babies are lovely.

I turned up the corners of my mouth. It was expected of me.

"I have to go get her," Maryann said and turned to Steve. "Are you sure she'll come with me?"

There was always that doubt about Sally.

Maryann went to change into something that would make her look less pudgy as if pudginess would thwart her purpose with Sally, and as if there exists an outfit capable of transforming a pudgy body into a supermodel. I followed her into our bedroom.

"Steve is different, you know," was the first thing she said to me.

She wiggled into the new gabardine slacks with the special tummy control panel in front.

"No, I didn't know. Listen, Maryann..."

"I think they want you for the whole weekend. Louis said…."

"Louis! You call him Louis?"

"That's what he said to call him." She giggled. "He kissed my hand. Isn't he precious?"

"He's a killer, Maryann. There's nothing precious about him."

She stuck a round, magenta earring into her earlobe. It matched some of the flowers printed on her blouse.

"I know he's probably dangerous," she said. "But it's hard to imagine. He's so charming. It seems Sally and Danny are in some kind of trouble. They're helping to protect them. Isn't that sweet?"

"By bringing them here? By having you bring them here?"

How sweet.

"Steve says they must not touch their minivan, you know, the silver one. He says there is information that there may be a car bomb. I had no idea Steve had such terrible enemies. Why do you suppose that is?"

I had not told her about the airliner he shot down as an Air Force fighter pilot. I told her now.

"How horrible!" She shook her head, deploring the world as it is. "When I answered the door, Steve pushed his way in and Louis was right behind him. You will help, won't you Leo? Louis said they will need you to stay at the safehouse. He will give you the address."

She put on her mascara by holding the wand steady and blinking her eyelashes down across it. Next came lipstick. She puckered up and put some of it on my cheek on her way out.

The Frenchman chuckled when I gave a last longing look at the half martini still in my glass. He swallowed the rest of his before he left my kitchen and my home. Then Steve and I had a little talk in the laundry room and he told me the score. As with everything else in Steve's life, it began with a fight.

TWO

Steve Donovan is a pretty medium sort of guy. He's medium height and medium weight, with medium brown hair, maybe too much of that, or am I just jealous? Anyway, he has a lot of brown hair that he doesn't always keep well-trimmed and more than medium brown eyes with eyelashes almost like a girl's. This combination earned him the Section nickname Bear.

The token Woman in The Section, which I run, dubbed him that, and gave him a lot of her attention, as women generally do with Steve. He hates the name, but I don't think he minds the attention.

The point is that you wouldn't expect this middle-roader to be a black belt, multiple degrees, in several different styles of martial arts, but he is. He spends much of his free time at it, as he was on the day off I gave him that Friday. He told me he was attending a class in what he called the dojang that morning, having a normal workout, probably beating up one of those big bags that hang from the ceiling, bags that look soft and moveable but are deceptively filled with cement.

Steve turned on instinct when two men came in through the office and sat down in the spectator section. He didn't hear them, he told me, he felt them. They were, of course, Mack and Louis (the Frenchman). They wore suits with ties that were not out of place in a political town like this but did not belong in a karate studio.

The dobok and black belt Charlie wore when he came in did belong, though, and Steve introduced him to his sensei. Everybody was polite. The sensei asked Charlie who his teacher was. Vasily Sobieski, Charlie replied. The instructor didn't think he knew the name. Would he and Steve like to spar?

"Sure," Charlie said.

"What did you say?" I asked Steve when he told me this.

"What the fuck was I supposed to say? No, thank you, it looks like you're here to kill me? Or how about, no, I'd rather have your father over there spectating quietly slit my throat. Shit, Frank. I said sure. Just like Charlie said."

"You thought they were there to take you out?"

"It crossed my mind. They don't make social calls, do they? My mind ran a fast search through the list of The Families trying to find one that might be able to afford to commission them."

The Families was Steve's name for the relatives and friends of people on the airliner he shot down who had sworn vengeance. Steve had been dodging a few handy accidents lately.

"And?" I asked him. "Could any of them afford Charle-magne?"

"No." He shrugged. "Besides, I beat the shit out of Charlie."

I was surprised. "You mean he's not very good?"

"He's fucking great. I'm just better. That's all."

But that wasn't all. I could tell by his tone. I waited.

"Charlie made me look good," he said finally. "In front of the other two. It's a kind of test, Frank, and I've passed the preliminaries."

I looked at him standing there in my laundry room that Friday evening. It was one of our few opportunities to talk privately. He pressed buttons on the washing machine, punched them like they were the enemy. He knew then and I knew then that death is not the only dramatic change that can occur in a life.

"How do you know you passed?" I asked him.

He smiled. "Mack told me I fight like Vasily."

THREE

I checked my back as I drove to the safehouse, circling the route three times to look for watchers. I never saw them. Steve rode with the team, a fact which even in my then-ignorant state I marked as significant, and he told me later they were behind me the whole time. Watching my back was the excuse—no doubt as preparation for shooting me in it. But I never saw them. Their tradecraft is that good.

The place was as generic as safehouses come. I didn't know who had set it up for them. They have networks I am only dimly aware of, and they carefully hid the local one from me. As generics go, the suburbs, the streets, and the neighborhood of this house, even the late summer day, participated in studied plainness. Green lawns and trees ran to olive drab, showing up against the bleached sky without defining lines. It reminded me of Southeast Asia, where everything melted into the booby-trapped landscape. It was maybe not as hot here, but it felt every bit as deceptive and dangerous.

I walked into the house. It smelled like a safehouse. That is to say, there was strong coffee brewing. I helped myself and thought about that half martini I was missing and all my wife's tales of a harmless (to me, but not to her) day's adventures at the coffee morning, the women's book club, the charity bazaar planning committee. Every event sans the Frenchman and his charms.

The team came in behind me. Louis, as usual, swept for bugs right away, forcing us all to chat mindlessly to keep any devices actively transmitting. There were none and he went outside to set up the perimeter sensors, infrared and motion, and took Steve with him. I had never been allowed to observe the details of their security measures. Steve was not only watching; he was being instructed.

That left me standing by the coffee pot staring at the two assassins who blamed me for the loss of wife/mother and daughter/sister less than a year before. Our conversation was more than a little strained, to say the least. In monosyllables, Charlie told me to shut up and wait for a general explanation when Steve and Louis returned.

I drank my coffee.

We gathered like one big happy family at a wobbly kitchen table with twisted metal legs and a white Formica top. It matched the metal and Formica of the kitchen cabinets. The place looked more than commonly institutional. It must be an FBI dive, I thought.

Mack spoke to Steve. I was being allowed to listen but not formally acknowledged as a participant. I was under the increasing impression I was expected to play a role, that my play in this game would require sacrifice, and it would be more than half a martini's worth. I knew I would never be compensated for it, not even to the extent of a simple thank you, but staying alive would be plenty thanks for me.

Mack's Austrian German was as slurpy as ever and I watched Steve struggle to take it in at least as fast as he sometimes can manage good old *hoch Deutsch*, which is to say, not very fast. A government investigation into government corruption gets quicker results.

I've listened to Mack for almost twenty years, so I was able later, when we were alone again briefly, to fill Steve in on the details he missed due to language.

"We have information," Mack told Steve, "that Five-Fifths has a commission on your family."

Always up on the news, Steve said, "Who the fuck is Five Fifths?"

Where did he get the vocabulary? And in two languages?

Charlie answered. "Five-Fifths is a new team. They got their start in the IRA, but are civilians now, operating privately. Their clients are predictable, all bargain basement payers. The team is not good enough yet to demand high fees, but their bomber shows potential. They are becoming noticed."

Steve took all this in, more or less. Charlie's English is American, but his Deutsch is as Austrian as his papa's. Steve swallowed hard and asked in German which made Mack wince—made us all wince—"Who commissioned them?"

"The name is Lorese," said Mack.

I thought I could see a scroll of names running through Steve's mind's eye listing The Families who wanted him, and his, dead.

"They are not one of the usuals," he told Mack.

"No. They are Creoles, living in Surinam. There was an old and distant uncle on that airplane."

Steve was full of questions, crowded in his throat, clamoring to be let out first so they all stuck in the doorway of his mouth making it open and shut three times before one finally squeezed past the others and made its way into intelligible language.

"What do you propose?"

"We propose nothing. This is your affair."

"But you're here. You saved my life. I saw the C4 in my car's wheel well. My wife, my son…."

Charlie interrupted, "What do you want to do, Steve?"

I watched my subordinate's face. I had to. I was losing friends and associates at an astonishing rate this year and here was the latest. Does one become an operational specialist at the first drop of blood, or before then, when the trigger is squeezed. Or does it happen even earlier, at the point of decision?

"I want to kill the mother fuckers," he said.

There are some sticky philosophical problems here. On the one hand, Steve is hunted. I know that my natural reaction in such a case would be to defend myself. Steve is better at that than I would be, and offense is always the best defense. On the other hand, Steve is guilty as sin of the crime for which he is hunted. I like to think I would pay for such a crime, gladly, but then, I'm guilty of helping, in my own careless, bureaucratic way, in the deaths of Mack's wife and daughter, and I am not asked to pay, except in the stony silence of broken acquaintance. Why should I expect Steve to pay? Under whose law? While I can claim the vagaries of bureaucracy, loyalty, and obedience to authority in my defense, so can Steve.

Sally and the baby should need no defense, but they are targets by association. I still have three children at home. The sight of Mack and Charlie in front of my house sent a convulsion of fear through me. I was ready to run the charming Frenchman through with a lance over one pudgy middle-aged woman who mixes great martinis and puts on makeup before going out to rescue the threatened.

Sure, I can condemn Steve's decision. I just can't say I wouldn't have done the same.

So we sat around the table as Steve metamorphosed into a killer and I caught Mack watching me as it sunk in. He turned away quickly.

"Do you want the family dead, too?" was Charlie's next question.

Steve's brow wrinkled. "Of course not. Is it even verified they commissioned it?"

Louis smiled. "No."

"I didn't think so," said Steve. "It's all wrong. They aren't one of The Families; they're too conveniently far away. The old uncle is not even a close connection. No, I want Five Fifths, not the Loreses."

"But somebody is paying Five Fifths," said Louis, always the first to bring up finances.

"Who?"

He shrugged.

"Let's find out." Steve sounded just like Louis, despite his bad Deutsch.

"And then?"

"And then…." Steve's turn to shrug.

There was work to be done before we could find out anything. I got on the horn and lined up all the green stamps I had saved over the years, preparing to cash them in for a toaster oven that would probably burn down my house someday soon. Not that I'm saying Steve's not worth it, or that I don't owe Mack. He is and I do, but that doesn't make it easier to part with one's life savings in favors for a hopeless cause.

When all my ducks had lined up neatly in a row, I turned to what was going on in our humble safehouse, to the domestic tranquility that might very well be possible when only scotch and black coffee are available, but I doubt it. Charlie and Steve were gone. Where? I wanted to know. To watch Steve's car, I was told. Lucky stiffs, I thought, and they'll be so stiff by morning after such an exciting night that the young bully will no doubt take it out on me. I did not know which young bully I meant.

Louis stayed busy at the green screen of a new personal computer, glaring at me every time I tried to have a peek at what he was doing. I didn't see anything precious in the way he sloshed coffee over the carpet or complained about lousy American food.

I sat on the sofa and knew it was a mistake, but had no excuse to move to the hard, straight-backed chair I would need to stay awake. Mack sat in an easy chair, watching a sensor screen flashing green dots at him from a briefcase on his lap. I stared at him unwillingly, asleep with my eyes open, until little bells going off in what was left of my common sense warned me he was staring back at me.

I guess I closed my eyes soon after that and laid my head half on the back of the sofa and half on my shoulder. My neck froze in that position, stretching one side and shrinking the other so that sitting up became a painful contortion, but I had to get to my feet fast. Mack was kicking me in the shin, not hard enough to break it, but hard enough, and saying something about 'having them.' I heard Charlie's voice coming over the radio, reciting street names.

"Go wake Louis," said Mack. In German it was even shorter, only two words instead of three.

I hit the corner of the wall as I stumbled into the short hallway, bruising my shoulder and making what I hoped was enough noise to wake the Frenchman before I got to the door. People with reflexes like his are not safe to wake up. I reached the bedroom door, knocked, and cleared my throat. I opened the door slowly, careful not to stand directly in the doorway, then looked inside and reached my hand in, feeling along the wall to turn on the light.

The Frenchman was sprawled diagonally across a double bed, completely dressed, except for his jacket. His tie was loosened and his shirt sleeves rolled up. One arm was flung up over his eyes.

Surely the bastard wasn't going to make me come in and shake him. He had to be awake. I noticed the way his shirt and belt met in the middle smoothly, without overlap by one or the other, both looking expensive, and the whole effect being one of well, but not over, fed health.

I'd look like that—well, I wouldn't be as tall—if I worked out several hours a day the way these guys did. But I have a living to make, food and shelter to provide for four other people, college tuition for three more, and I'm still paying for the wedding of another one. That means I have to spend most waking hours in a windowless box reading reports by fluorescent light in between brief episodes of gut-wrenching terror, testing heart-attack theories by drinking whole pots of strong coffee.

I stepped into the room and cleared my throat again. The bastard was being his old charming self all right. I sighed and walked up to the bed, reached a hand toward his shoulder, and stopped when he said, "What?"

...

I never use my vehicles for things like this, mostly because things like this are rarely conducted in my own country, this being another agency's jealously guarded turf, but circumstances dictated otherwise and the three of us climbed into my car after checking for booby traps.

Circumstances are tricky things, and the one that led me to delay buying a new alternator in July was particularly unlucky. Strong prayer got the car started anyway. Mack did not look at me, staring straight ahead through the windshield as I cranked the engine, but his lips were so tightly compressed, they threatened to turn white. I could hear the precious Louis sneering through his teeth at me from the back seat. The car ran fine once it started.

The radio Mack held crackled. He turned up the volume, and Steve gave us directions to the Five-Fifths safehouse.

FOUR

I knew when I turned off the ignition that it was not going to start again. There was nothing I could do. The neighborhood was unfriendly. My companions were unfriendly. Five-Fifths, the most unfriendly of all, had holed themselves up in an industrial complex, between a restaurant supply and an auto body shop. The entrance to their lair was a rolling metal door, truck-sized, in a concrete wall.

I parked on the next block and had to tell Mack and Louis before they left that the car wasn't going to start again. They were checking their weapons at the time, preparing to run to the rendezvous with the other two, and my news was unwelcome. Mack's blue eyes did plenty of cutting into my ego. He told me, in syllables, to go to their car, an ill-fitting BMW, on the other side of the industrial site.

It took me twenty minutes to get there by a roundabout way. It was a humid night and I was sweating. I could not touch the car; the alarms were set in a way only they knew, and if I disturbed them, the car would be unusable. Disturbing them for no reason also would be useless to me. I didn't have the keys. So I shivered in a doorway as the night temperature dropped and condensation formed on my scalp. I had to be careful to stay out of the view of security cameras on the industrial buildings around me. I listened for footsteps.

I had used up twenty minutes in getting there, and it was another twenty before I heard what I wanted: running footsteps, two sets, no, four. How many men were in Five Fifths? I tried to remember. Five, or six? Six. They wouldn't run to the car if they were the victors. They wouldn't know about this car any more than they would know about the broken one two blocks away. And they couldn't care less about a shivering babysitter in a doorway. I shrank back a little anyway. I could see my belt buckle catching the light from a security lamp across the street. It glittered like a beacon.

Charlie threw the car keys at me. "You drive, Frank."

I had to take my hand off my Walther PPK to catch the keys, which is a good thing because fingering my old friend was a self-preservation gesture that could have killed me. Louis had seen my hand inside my coat and I was already looking down the barrel of his Modèle 1935. From my angle, it seemed his night sights were centered just above my nose.

"Where?" I asked as I started the engine.

"It doesn't matter," said Charlie. "Drive around and check our back."

He was my passenger. Steve sat squashed between Mack and Louis in the back seat. The car was not roomy. It was a BMW, not their usual Mercedes, with no armor, and the radios were mounted improperly, sliding around under the gear shift. I felt a little smug as I considered the obvious failings of whomever they had suborned into providing this piece of junk. I always provided more than adequate vehicles.

There was some catching of breath, after their, shall we say, exertions, and then the run to the car. They smelled of cordite. In the rearview mirror, I saw the Frenchman's eyes move constantly under the street lights, watching for bogeymen in the streets. He turned every few minutes to stare behind us. Charlie gave me continuous directions for back-checking and losing tails, and it took all my strength to seal my lips so I would not blurt out—to my guaranteed detriment—what I thought about having some kid teach me my trade. Their tradecraft is superb, but he didn't tell me anything I didn't already know, and if he did, I missed it, as I would not have done if his father had said it.

After ten minutes of turns, stops and starts on a humid night, and maybe there were other reasons, old iron-stomach Steve spewed.

He'd had a few donuts and a lot of coffee. Much of it soaked Mack's pant leg. Louis protested loudly. I swerved to pull off the road, and they rushed to get Steve out of the car, but he was already finished and it was pooled on the floor on both sides of the hump in the back, inching its way forward under the front seats. They put Steve in a window seat then, and Mack made him ride doubled over, saying this would help, but breathing it all in with such close proximity only gave him the dry heaves. We opened all the windows because we were all in danger, and Mack finally let Steve sit up and breathe air.

"Is there anything back at that warehouse that I should be taking care of?" I asked with a casual air.

"Like what?" Charlie gave me an innocent look.

"Like bodies. Evidence. Police. That sort of thing."

"Is that what you do?" asked Charlie. "I thought you just made bad coffee. I suppose there must be a reason for your existence."

I squashed the sudden urge to throttle the brat.

"There is a phone." He pointed to the console between us, where a box slid back and forth between the seats. "Use it."

"I'm driving," I reminded him. "And at any rate, I have to be there, I can't take you with me, and I don't have a car."

There were a few moments of silence, like a memorial to lost babysitters everywhere, and then the Frenchman said, "Your wife has a car."

"How the hell do you know what my wife has?" It was out before I could stop it. Of course, my wife had to take something to collect Sally and the baby, and only a moron would not be able to deduce from that fact that she had her own car, as does any other American woman in our socioeconomic class, another telling fact to the average moron, and of course, Louis is no moron. But he had no business even thinking about my wife. I saw his eyebrows rise in the rearview mirror, and he fired off a significant glance to his side, where Mack no doubt returned it.

FIVE

"Really, Leo, I can't believe you would do such a silly thing." She swabbed the knot on my forehead. "What made you do it?" I looked around. I was in my bedroom, on my bed. My wife was wrapping a washcloth around an ice cube. She put it on the bump. She wore the brocade bathrobe I gave her for her birthday, the one from the sexy lingerie store at the mall.

"Who brought me up here?" I asked.

"Steve and Charlie."

I remembered lunging for the Frenchman. "Did I hit him?"

"No," she said.

"Did he hit me?" I did not remember seeing him move.

"No. He moved away and you fell forward into the washing machine." She went to her closet. "Nobody's ever kissed my hand before, Leo," she called from the racks. "I wish you hadn't spoiled it. I'm not used to such gallant manners. I was enjoying it."

Evidently. "He's very polite when he shoots people, always says *may I*." I took the ice cube off my head and threw it at the closet door.

She came out wearing a magenta jogging suit and wrinkled her little nose at me. "You keep saying that," she said. "But I can't imagine it."

"Try. There are six examples of his work in an industrial park a few miles down the highway. I have to go clean it up. I need to get on the phone with Chief Harkon and then I'll take your keys. My car's dead. We'll pick it up tomorrow morning."

"Louis killed six people?"

"He helped."

I stood up, fought down the spinning sensation, then the nausea, pulled her into my arms, and buried my sore head in her dark chestnut hair. I crushed one side of her 'do'. She impatiently plumped it back out with her fingers, but she smiled at me and kissed my bruise gently.

"I didn't see Pete's car in the drive," I said. Pete is our eldest son still at home.

"He and Michael are staying at the wrestling coach's house tonight. They have a match in the morning." Maryann opened the bedroom door and shepherded me out.

I nodded. Michael is our youngest son still at home. I was glad the boys were not in the house. That left Theresa, my daughter, to worry about. A big enough worry.

From the top of the stairs, I heard voices in the kitchen. "My God! They're still here!"

"Yes, of course, Leo. They're hungry. I told them to help themselves."

Downstairs, I heard the refrigerator door close, the clink of plates and utensils, and a feminine giggle. I counted on help from Steve, but he wasn't there. Mack and Louis sat at the kitchen table, drinking coffee and eating coffee cake. Charlie leaned casually across the counter, smiling at my daughter. He was no more than a foot away from her, as she built a hoagie on a baguette, using everything available in the house, from mayonnaise to my favorite Genoese salami. She giggled at something Charlie was saying to her as I stormed in.

"Where the hell is Steve?" I demanded of Charlie.

I wanted his eyes off my daughter's legs. He had been slyly stealing glances at her thighs. She wore jogging shorts and a cropped college sweatshirt. Her dark brown wedge haircut was messy, but only in the most becoming way. There was mascara on her eyelashes, the little vixen, but nothing covered the sprinkle of freckles across her nose.

Charlie paused and gave me the same blue-eyed X-ray stare I'd had so many times from his father. "Steve is in the garage, cleaning the car." It was a calm, matter-of-fact answer, delivered in a way that heightened the contrast between his state and mine. "Are you going to attack the sink the same way you did the washing machine, Frank?"

"You son of a bitch, she's eighteen!" I probably shouted this. I've been told I did.

Maryann came in behind me saying, "Shhh! The neighbors!"

Charlie answered me with a very cold, "My sister would have been fifteen this month."

Simultaneously, Theresa said, "Dad!" but in a way that it took much longer than a three-letter, single-syllable word should take to be said and heard. My wife, meanwhile, repeated her theories about the neighbors.

"Go to your room!" I told Theresa.

Maryann sounded like a snake with her shushing. Louis laughed. Steve's wife, Sally, came in from the garage wearing a pair of wet rubber gloves and carrying a bucket that stank. She shouted something about some men being beyond all help and tossed the contents of the bucket down the sink drain, which set Theresa off about the knife there that she wanted to use to cut the sandwich. I repeated my order to Theresa. She defied me with a loud "No!" and gave Sally a dirty look.

My wife found her another knife for the sandwich and delivered it with a lecture on manners. Louis roared with laughter. Sally filled the bucket again and sloshed it through the kitchen, then the laundry room, and finally out the door to the garage, which she slammed. Charlie deliberately ran a finger lightly over the skin of my daughter's leg, and if I'd had chest pains then, my sense of doom could not have been greater.

I was shouting at the top of my lungs now, and could feel it, could feel that my eyes were not blinking because they burned, could feel my hand reaching toward the gun I had never used except to qualify once a year, reaching hope-lessly I knew, because Charlie was so much faster, so much more accurate, so much deadlier than I am that it was no match. I was going to die. But by God, I had to....

"Michael."

It was said quietly, in German. It made the whole room quiet because, until that moment, Mack had said nothing. He followed the single word with a significant look.

I thought, at first, he was talking about my son, *auf Deutsch*. Had the boy come home? No. Mack meant his own son. Charlie's real name is Michael. Charlie, aka Michael, snatched his hand away from my daughter's leg like it had been burned by dry ice and he couldn't detach it fast enough without leaving behind skin from his fingers. He lowered his eyes, looked away from mine, extinguished the defiance. He took his other hand out of his coat, off the Glock in its hol-ster, and sat at the table, across from his father, away from my daughter, eyes down.

I was impressed. My daughter was still slicing the sandwich. I took my hand away from my gun and grasped Theresa's arm to propel the disobedient child from the room. My wife restrained me. I admit it would have been undigni-fied, but I was shamed into wanting some obedience, even at the cost of a scene.

Mack defused this, too. "You have something to do," he said, looking at me only briefly, only long enough to get the words out and make them imperative.

SIX

"They're all slimy. And he's the slimiest. He looks like a frog, a lumpy, bald frog, and if that's what you think you're married to, that and the sneaky, dirty job that man does, then have at it. I'm not going with you, and neither is Danny."

Sally turned at the sound of the door shutting behind me. I was in the garage now, standing on the little step at the door to the laundry room. The BMW was in front of me, my wife's car parked on the other side of it. Sally and Steve stood between them. She had been speaking with some heat and was breathing hard. He had that blank look that I've tried myself once or twice, never successfully, the external evidence of an internal war against committing oneself to any certain action in an uncertain situation. His mouth was open slightly. He was doing a good job of looking unintelligent.

I cleared the rear bumper of the beamer before they moved. It was a poignant moment. Then, Sally threw a sponge into the bucket between them, splashing Steve's pants, and stomped past him and around the front of the car. She slammed the laundry room door shut behind her.

I might have paid more attention to being called slimy if my mind were not so full of Theresa. Justice where it is due, Charlie is everything a father looks for in a daughter's suitor. He is rich, educated, and intelligent (one does not always follow the other), and he looks respectable. She would find him handsome, no doubt, with his blue eyes and blond hair, perfect build, and he's witty, oh yes, very witty. All of that, except that he kills for a living. He kills bad guys, other killers, society's pathogens, but he kills, and in the end, that's all he does, like a poison called medicine, a human chemotherapy.

I remembered another babysitter's daughter, Alexandra Dolnikov, daughter of my old boss Fred. Now she's the widow of Vasily Sobieski, the team's dead explosives expert. I wondered about her for a moment, locked up somewhere with her child for safety, protected by Mack, Louis, and Charlie. She was not much older than Theresa is now when she first met Sobieski. I'd been pretty smug when I told Fred the score back then.

"Listen!" Steve and I said it together. Then we said, again together, "You first."

I went first because I'm the boss. But I forgot what I was going to say. "You sure know how to impress a new boss, Steve. I'm glad you didn't throw up on me."

The car door was open. It oozed a sick smell mixed with pine cleaner. Steve's brow wrinkled. "New boss? I suppose so." He played with the door, swinging it on its hinges, like a fan, to dry the wet carpet, as an exercise in futility.

I put my hands in my pockets and shuffled my feet.

"I'm on my way to the scene," I said.

He nodded. "Did you call Chief Harkon?"

My turn to nod. "Was it bad?"

He shrugged. "Pretty gruesome. But fast. And the tangos were all scumbags. There's that at least." He stopped swinging the door. "I never got sick in an airplane."

"Listen, Steve, Sally…."

He interrupted me. "She didn't mean… she's upset."

"No, I know. She'll come with you. Give her time."

He shrugged again. "They don't pick up their brass, Buddy. I tried to pick up mine. It's all U.S.-made, while theirs is Austrian. It's probably not a good idea for me to be linked to this—in my position, that is."

"You resigned your position yesterday, Steve."

"Thanks, Buddy. I knew you'd take care of it. Should I turn in my weapon before I leave?"

"Do I want it?"

He thought for a moment. "No. You don't. I'll dispose of it—later."

My turn to say thanks. "Did you find all your brass?"

"No," he said. "I missed two."

Great. This was going to be delicate. My own home-
town, my personal friend the police chief present, and two
stray pieces of all-American residue amid dozens of foreign
shells to find and dispose of without telling Harkon why. If
it's not political, he will say, why worry about it being traced
to your office? He doesn't know what my office does. Not
many people do. It doesn't function in full sunlight.

"Have they said anything? Have they told you why
they're bringing you on the team?" I wanted to ask him if he
knew what he was doing. I restrained myself.

Steve leaned over the door window, resting his chin on
his forearm. The door squeaked under his weight. "I'm Charlie's project," he said. "Mack approves and Louis is amused. I
think it has to do with Alex."

Here was intelligence, juicy, grade-A prime, vitamin en-
riched, and I'd been dieting too long. I wanted details. I
wanted to know how Steve had figured this out. Then I remembered that forgotten thought.

"Speaking of babysitters' daughters, Steve...."

He closed the car door and smiled. "I'll try, but Charlie's
pretty fast." He picked up the bucket. "I'd better go."

We both said, "Right" at the same time.

SEVEN

Home again after meeting Chief Harkon.

"Where are they?" I asked.

"They went to the safehouse," said Maryann. "They said you know where it is. The blond man said they couldn't sleep here. The older blond one. The young one kissed Theresa in the laundry room. She's on cloud nine. But then Steve came in and stopped him, said he owes it to a friend who is out on a limb for him."

Maryann took a breath at last as she put a cup of black coffee in front of me, next to the remnants of a miserable sliver of coffee cake left over from her generous hospitality of a few hours ago. I was about to protest the depredation of all my comforts, but she continued.

"So the young one, that would be Charlie—isn't he just a doll, Leo? Charlie told Steve that a woman is a sufficient test of any friendship, and then his father told him something in German, so he sat down and ate the sandwich Theresa made for him. She says she'll never speak to Steve again, for stopping the most wonderful kiss in her life."

"In her whole, long life." I said it to the crumbs on my plate.

Maryann sat beside me at the kitchen table and frowned. "Is that blood on your sleeve?"

"Probably."

I'm not one of those secret squirrel types who never tells his wife anything and then wonders why she blabs significant details to the world, but I've always been careful to come home clean. Maryann knows my job is secret and maybe nasty, but there is a difference between simple knowledge and the full understanding that comes from experience. I watched it begin to dawn on her.

She pursed her lips to pose a question but it didn't come right away. Maybe it began as a who or a what question, but it came out finally as, "Not the young one, too? Not Charlie?"

I nodded.

"But he's so sweet."

I gagged.

She was thoughtful for a moment. "Sally and Steve have some real problems, Leo. I had a long talk with poor Sally. She's such a pretty girl."

Poor spoiled but pretty Sally.

I emptied my pockets onto the table. Maryann watched the brass roll out, handful by handful. She questioned me silently.

"Two of these are Steve's," I explained. "I couldn't very well tell Harkon what I was looking for, or why, so I had him help me pick them all up."

"Steve?"

"Yes."

"But not you, Leo?"

"What? Of course not."

"Thank God."

Even with the fresh memory of six men on their backs staring through their own blood at a factory ceiling, I felt, of all things, not gratitude, but regret. Was I so vain that I thought I should make that grade, too? I am a superb intelligence officer, a competent bureaucrat, a rare enough animal. What made me think I should want Steve's skill and Steve's invitation? I certainly didn't want Steve's enemies or his marital problems.

I tried to smile, to hide the momentary lapse.

"Did Mack say I was to come to the safehouse?" My feelings swung the other way now, toward a desire to be left completely out of it.

Maryann nodded. "He said there is information to sift through."

"I'm not surprised. There wasn't a scrap of paper in the place. Harkon had to take my word for who the corpses were. I told him about their one-time IRA affiliation. He concocted his own theory from that—a nice, plausible story of terrorist double crosses that is completely wrong but will make everybody happy. I let him believe it. The team had stripped away all the intelligence, as well as the explosive."

"Why would they do that?"

"They live on information. They get first dibs on all documents in most cases. It's usually part of the deal."

"But why would they keep the explosive?" Maryann reached for my hand and held it until I took it away to drink my coffee.

"High explosive is expensive." I showed her how empty my cup was. "And Louis is cheap."

"But he dresses so well," she said as she took my cup to the counter.

I mimed her words behind her back while she poured another cup.

"Does this have to do with that Air Force incident?" she asked. "Sally thinks it does. She has never forgiven him."

"A lot of people have never forgiven him."

"Are they the ones trying to kill him? Hiring thugs to blow him up. And Sally and the baby, too? For a mistake?"

"Mistakes can kill, Maryann. Someone has to be responsible. Why not the guy who pulled the trigger?"

"But the baby?"

"I agree that's excessive."

"So one of these families wants to add more atrocity to atrocity? It's atrocious!" She was very angry, rubbing the guts out of her special antique coffee cake dish with a towel, while my fresh cup of coffee grew cold on the counter. I didn't move from my spot at the table, though. It was a ring-side seat for watching this performance.

"I don't think it was one of the families this time," I said, because I wanted to stir her up a little more and because I really didn't think it was.

She threw the towel at the sink and missed. It slid to the floor. "Then who was it?" she demanded, hands on hips.

"That's what Mack is trying to find out."

"And when he does?"

I smiled as she picked up the towel. "He'll do what he does best."

I had the satisfaction of seeing her suppress a shudder.

EIGHT

Mr. Sweetie Pie lounged diagonally across the institutional sofa in the safehouse living room. Mr. Well Dressed was not in the room. "Louis will be very upset if you take your eyes off the sensors," Charlie told Steve. "You should not upset Louis."

Steve sat scowling in an armchair against the adjacent wall, watching the green screen on the coffee table before him, monitoring the sensors outside.

"Where are the others?" I asked.

Steve kept his eyes on the screen. "Asleep," he said.

Charlie didn't speak. Steve kicked him in the ankle, showing a whole new level of familiarity. I noted it with dread. "I know. I'm going to," said Charlie.

Going to what, Brat? I collapsed silently in the chair opposite him. I admit, my expression was not friendly.

He could do a pretty good unfriendly face, too. "Did you go home?" he asked me.

I glared.

"Did you see Sally? Did she say anything?"

Sally? I shook my head slowly. Maybe I was too tired to keep up with the thoughts of Sweetie Pie the Lightning Bolt.

"She has to come with you, Steve," said Charlie.

The bastard has designs on Sally!

Steve shook his head. "I'll do my best."

"Do better than that. Show some backbone. My father is after me to produce an heir, but what woman is willing to be locked up for life at Vasily's Carpet? You have an advantage. Sally is already your wife. You can make her come with you."

Steve looked away from the screen, and we both stared into Charlie's light blue eyes, so innocent, so virginal—in the face of certain realities.

"Spoken like a bachelor," said Steve. He looked back at the screen. "Is that what you call the place? Vasily's Carpet?"

Charlie nodded. "I could produce a bastard by Theresa. Do you think that would please my father?"

"Fuck, Charlie!" Steve kicked him again.

"What? Yes. She's delicious!"

"Mack said...."

"Call him Misha. His friends don't call him Mack." Charlie looked at me. "Why aren't you reaching for your Walther?"

"Because this is such an obvious provocation." I impressed myself with my cool tone. I was so far beyond enraged, it had a calming effect.

Charlie sighed. "I am instructed to assure you I won't make any bastards by your daughter. There is no reason for you to attempt suicide."

I looked at him lounging there, without his tie or jacket, the Glock in its holster showing black against his white shirt.

His talk was appropriate to the hour, a pre-dawn collection of sleepy nonsense.

"If you're anything like your father was at this age," I said, "I'll need a lot more than a half-promise not to get her pregnant."

He straightened up a little and opened his eyes wide. They were as bloodshot as mine. "If I am polite to you, will you give me details of my father at this age?"

He was a young carnivore, full of mischief.

"Papa is very moral now and has given up his mistress. So has Louis. They are both almost saintly. I find it unfair." Charlie raised his right hand. "I promise and give you my word as a gentleman, that I will not touch your daughter, Theresa, not even a little bit, nor at all, though I find her scrumptious and wonder how she is your daughter."

The fingers of his left hand were crossed. It was the best I was going to get.

He put his hand down and became very still like his father is before he kills. "My promise is good," said Charlie, "as long as you keep yours."

"Mine?

"Yes. The one about not writing any of this down or telling it to another soul."

"But I have to make a report...."

"It need not be lengthy, or true. I shall dream of Theresa." His meaning was pretty clear.

He looked at his watch and wagged a finger at me. "It's time to wake them up. I will make coffee." To Steve he said, "Be sure you are looking at that screen when Louis comes into the room. Stay on his good side. It is important."

Like any government fixture, the chair was not designed for comfort, but I found it a lot more comfortable than the thought of waking Mack and Louis. I stayed in it. Charlie stood up. "I told you to wake them up," he said.

"I don't take orders from kids."

I expected a blow, an attack of some kind, and would have welcomed the bruise as a badge of ultimate victory. I was disappointed.

He clamped his lips together and stared at me for a full half-minute. No threats, no movement at all, just that same still menace that gives me the creeps with his father. Finally, he said quietly, "In my father's absence, I am responsible. If you disagree, then you must take it up with him."

I made as much noise as possible going down the hall. I banged on the first bedroom door, then on the second, then prepared to enter the first room, carefully, and had my hand on the knob when the door flew open and I was on my stomach on the hallway floor, one arm twisted behind me, the other pinned at my side. The Frenchman sat on my legs. I shouted "It's me! It's me!"

Mack said something from somewhere behind me, and Louis laughed.

NINE

"Your son is disrespectful to his elders." I found myself alone with Mack at the kitchen table and this was my brilliant opener. I'm sure it was lack of sleep that put me off my usual stride.

Mack's eyebrows came up a fraction. "Your daughter should not display her legs in that fashion."

"American boys are taught enough manners to keep their hands to themselves."

"Then your Michael is as much a foreigner here as mine." He pulled a wrinkled piece of paper from his shirt pocket.

"My Michael?"

"He spent the evening with a girl."

"He was at his coach's house."

"I have the report here." He smoothed the paper on the table. "It seems his coach has a porch in front of the house. And a daughter."

"You had them watched?"

"You know my methods." He shoved the paper toward me. "It is a quaint American term, necking."

"You don't have to do this. I have not been able to say it before, but I am sorry about what happened to your family, and I am heartily sorry for the role I played in it. You don't have to make me sorrier by threatening my family."

"I have not threatened your family." He looked positively offended. He needed a shave and his tie was missing, his shirt open at the neck. The leather of his holster was gleaming black, worn over the shoulders and across the back so that his SIG Sauer nestled under his arm. He scowled, disgusted with me. "When did I threaten them?"

"Your very presence. You have to admit...."

"When did I commit such an atrocity as you suggest? In your experience? When?"

"I've heard ...."

"When?"

"Never in my experience."

He leaned against the wall, still scowling. We stared across the table at each other in silence for a few minutes and, for the first time, communicated, though silently. You son of a bitch, he said to me without speaking, why the hell didn't you destroy those pictures?

I ask myself that every day, I told him without words. The regret is unbearable.

So many years! His eyes shouted at me. I saved your miserable neck countless times and could not depend on you to bend one bureaucratic rule to protect my family?

I know, I know. I'm breaking them all now. See? I covered up the killing last night. I fiddled with the computer to release Steve to you. *I'm here, breaking all the rules now.*

"Why am I here?" I asked him aloud.

"When we discover who hired Five-Fifths, you must commission the execution."

"You expect to find him here?"

"Yes, of course."

I'm pretty sharp, brilliant, in fact, but I wasn't following this. "It wasn't one of The Families?" I said.

"No." He took his coat from behind his chair and began going through the pockets, throwing a half dozen passports and a couple of thin wallets in my direction. Then he reached into the corner beside the microwave cabinet, pulled out a briefcase, put it on the table, and opened it. It was full of cash.

"It is one hundred thousand," he said. "And only a down payment. The Families offer as much, but not up front, and not in dollars. This was a big commission for Five-Fifths. Unfortunately, they did not survive it. They were not rogues; they were strictly political. Working without a babysitter would have been unthinkable to them. It would ruin their reputation. They were intent upon building it."

"So there is a babysitter somewhere," I said as I stared at the passport picture of a dead man. "And The Families could not provide a babysitter." It was an American passport, a professional-looking forgery. "But whoever commissioned it used the airline incident as cover." I was thinking out loud, and just let it roll. "Yes," I said. "The commission on Sally and the baby is just a cover for getting Steve. But why? Not that he doesn't have plenty of friends who hate him. What about the FBI man, Turner? Did he give you this safehouse by the way? It isn't one of mine. Turner and Steve never really got along."

"It is not Turner," said Mack. "He is not barbarous enough to kill from simple animosity. Killing like this needs something more: greed, hate, fear, revenge, jealousy, or worst of all, political policy. But like Turner, the killer must know that Steve shot down that airplane."

"That's not hard. It was in all the papers."

"But Steve uses his game name exclusively now. The killer must know both his real name and the new one, his history, and his present."

I put my head in my hands and stared at that nearly perfect American passport. "And he must know how to hire a specialist team," I said. "He must provide a babysitter. He must, in fact, be in my Section." *Oh God, not again.* I looked up. "You're not suspecting me?"

Mack closed the briefcase, irritated. "Of course not."

"Then why? Why do you want me to commission the execution of one of my subordinates?"

He leaned toward me. "Steve learned disobedience through disaster. He must now learn obedience. Blindly following rules is dangerous, but without them we are barbarians."

"He is becoming a specialist." I didn't think that was too far off barbarian.

"He is already operational. I must get control of him quickly, or he will be unmanageable."

"Unmanageable! You guys were never manageable. I don't have any hair because of all the times you made me pull it out. Fred told me he was promoting me when he assigned me to you, but he didn't say I might not live to enjoy it."

"Fred? Feodor Dolnikov?"

"The same. He assigned me to you. Gave me a cigar, the most terrible cigar ever made, to celebrate the occasion. He had a gross of the awful things. They were famous in The Section. He bought them when his kid was born and still had them ten years later because he couldn't get rid of them. People would take one out of politeness and then put it back in the box when he wasn't looking."

"His kid? Do you mean Alex?" There was a smile of sorts, around his mouth and behind the blue eyes.

"Yes. Alex. I still have that cigar, somewhere."

Then a real smile broke out. It is the only time I have ever seen him truly smile. He's got perfect teeth and no dimples, but all the mischief of his son times two. It made me forget who he is and what he is and it disappeared when the Frenchman walked into the room.

TEN

"You know, your English is slipping," I told The Brat. "It's not as perfect as it was last Christmas."

"I have not had opportunity to use it with someone who can corrects me. Alex is too busy since my mother died. She organizes the house now, and the household accounts."

"Can correct. I can correct you and will be happy to be of service."

"I will be happy if you shutted up."

I stared through the windshield at a clump of weeds. It was late morning on a drizzling Saturday. The humidity made itself into water and stuck mud to everything. This was lucky cover for my wife's otherwise noticeably pink minivan. The Frenchman balked at getting into it but was persuaded when he realized he would spend most of his time outside anyway. He preferred lying in the mud beside a telephone junction box. Charlie and I sat dry and ridiculous in a pink car nestled in a clump of weeds. We could see the target mobile home fifty yards to our left. There was a light on in the kitchen even in daytime, because the day was so grey.

Steve and Mack drove by in a jalopy.

"Where's the beamer?" I asked on the radio.

"We left it back there when we stole this one."

Great. I rested my forehead on the steering wheel.

"Household accounts?" I said to Charlie. "Do those contain the expenditures for mistresses?"

Charlie whistled softly. "Papa said you were good."

The jalopy pulled over in front of the target house.

"As I recall," I said, "Alex is not particularly pretty."

"There are other qualities more valuable than beauty." It was not merely a recitation. The kid was serious.

"For example?"

"There is the ability to live at Vasily's Carpet. We are not easy to live with."

"We're going in." It was Steve's voice on the radio.

"I always thought Alex was a bookish girl," I said. "Do you think she'll like Sally?"

He winced. "I think they will fight like cats."

Steve and Mack climbed out of their stolen car dressed in stolen clothes. They both wore torn, greasy blue jeans and black tee shirts decorated with skeletons and guitars and Olde English lettering dripping blood. They knocked on the front door of the target house.

Louis came back to the car, trailing a wire leading to a parabolic mic he had attached to a pole and carrying his equipment under one arm. The drizzle had become rain and soaked him to the skin. His black hair streamed down over his face in waves and ringlets. He climbed in the back swearing. I had been working on my French, so I knew the words he used.

"Testing, one, two, three," Steve said over his wire. He and Mack wore their mics under the t-shirts.

"Be quiet." Mack's wire worked, too.

The door opened and they went in.

The whole morning had been preparation for this culminating moment. We began by fine-tooth combing Five-Fifths' effects, coming across a little personal phone book. Bad form, to keep such a book. It even had phone numbers in it. All the numbers were European, complete with country codes, and Mack kept the book for later but gave Steve the engrossing occupation of reading each and every entry, one by one.

He found a number, without a name, scribbled sideways in a margin, and behold! It was a local number. The Frenchman got on the phone, calling someone—I suspected it was Turner—who broke into the phone company's computer and obtained the address of this one local phone number found on the body of a dead former terrorist turned specialist. We sat in the drizzle and watched that address for two hours. It was this slightly dilapidated single-wide trailer in front of us, past the weeds.

The occupants were a common law couple, man and girlfriend, who inhabited the same house but conducted separate lives. She was a part-time garment worker, discount auto parts store clerk, and temping receptionist. He, on the other hand, had no discernible occupation. From this, we surmised that he must be our target.

Charlie, Louis, and I watched through alternating drizzle and deluge. We would have liked to put a touch inside the house but could not think of a way to do it unobtrusively in daylight on a Saturday. We contented ourselves with wiring the phone and pointing a directional at the place. The television was on. The guy never budged. Unless he talked to himself, a touch on the house would not have yielded anything, anyway.

Mack and Steve had tracked the over-employed female, who was scheduled to be at the discount store that morning. She came home at eleven. We spent half an hour after that wondering where Steve and Mack were.

Mack told me later that Steve had done it all. The clothes came from a thrift store, the car from an apartment lot. Steve caught the lady's attention at her discount store, asking a series of questions about auto accessories that Mack didn't understand. Mack said Steve was flawless in every gesture, every nuance. He rolled his eyes at the ceiling; he snuffled; he even adjusted his pants at the crotch. The lady was captivated. Mack was impressed. *That's our boy.*

Steve told me later he felt he had passed another test.

"Yeah, hi," he said when she came to the door. "You left this." He handed her a wallet.

"Hey, thanks." She took the wallet. "What a bummer if I lost this, huh? You wanna come in? You wanna beer?"

"Yeah, sure."

The boyfriend was there in the living room, Steve told us later, on an old couch in his shorts and a torn tee shirt. The woman led them to the kitchen table, pointing to two un-matched rickety chairs. They sat down. We heard the scrapes on the floor over the wires.

"Yer all guys, so I ain't gonna tell him to put his pants on. I mean, you gotta be comfortable in yer own house, right?"

She was dressed in spandex shorts stretched over thick thighs and a sleeveless tunic that did not travel the same ground as her bra straps. Her bleached hair hung below her shoulders in broken lengths of wavy cascade, except for a tuft above her forehead that had been teased into an imita-tion of a cockscomb. For what reason, I didn't know. She wore full-length false fingernails painted with pumpkins for Labor Day. The paint job alone probably cost her more than her share of the rent. I can describe all this because I saw her later.

We heard the beers open and a bag rustle. "Try these," the woman said. "I got a good deal on 'em at Save U More. They're vinegar and blue cheese. Pretty good, huh?"

Crunches came from Mack and Steve in stereo. Mack said, in German, "These are the most vile things I have ever tasted."

"What'd he say?" she said. "That's not English, is it? Is it Spanish?"

"No. It's German. He said the chips are real good," said Steve.

"German! Wow! You speak all that stuff? I can only talk English."

"She speaks English," said Mack, "the way you speak German."

"What's he saying? Can you understand it, really?"

"He says he wants some more of them chips."

"Sure, honey." The bag rustled.

"You help me eat these, Steve, or I will stuff them down your throat."

"What'd he say? What'd he say?"

"He said thanks a lot."

"Yer welcome. How do you say yer welcome? Tell me how to say it so I can say it to him."

"Fick dich."

She practiced it once or twice before saying it to Mack. She shouted it, so he'd understand. It was at this point that I was glad Steve would be Mack's problem from now on. Back at the safehouse that night, he pounded a fist like a tree trunk into Steve's gut a couple of times to teach him respect.

I'm not allowed to do that to my subordinates in the civil service.

The guy on the sofa was the target, and Steve did his valiant best to start a conversation with him. Sonny In Shorts only grunted once or twice, in a friendly way, and watched the game on TV. I was beginning to take an interest in it myself.

We heard another beer can open. "Thanks," said Steve.

"You want a beer, Carl?" The lady shouted it over the TV commercial. "Shit. He's stoned. Look at that. Fucker's asleep. He's always asleep. You wanna go in my room and fuck, honey?"

We presumed she was talking to Steve.

"Bring him, too," she said. "Look at the size of them arms on him. He's kinda old for me, but if the rest of him looks like them arms, I can handle it. You can, like, translate."

There was a pause, then a crash, then a short scream, followed by the woman saying, "What the fuck?"

Steve briefed us later that she'd sat on his lap and reached into the front of his pants where the stock of his Smith & Wesson was digging into his gut. She was on the floor that fast, while Mack covered the sleeping boyfriend. Steve called for Charlie and Louis. I listened over the wires, in quadrophonic now, as they got down to business and worked over the boyfriend while the girlfriend wailed. After the first few blows, the woman made a run for it, but the Frenchman caught her.

The boyfriend said when he had the chance, "I dunno what the fuck you're talkin' about."

The woman was nearly hysterical. "Tell 'em, Carl. Tell 'em about that briefcase you brought to that phone booth."

"What briefcase? What the fuck you talkin' about, Cheryl? I don't know nothin' about no briefcase."

"You do, too. You took that briefcase to that phone booth, just like Brasser told you to, and you gave it to that guy, you know, that guy with the red hair and he said the code words like Brasser said...."

"Yer the one works for Brasser...." His words were cut off by the next blow.

It was Charlie who said, during an eerie silence while the boyfriend sucked air, "Tell me about Brasser, Cheryl."

"Doug Brasser. He works for the guy, the guy... don't hurt me. Please, don't hurt me. He works for this guy who helps my union. I run errands. He pays good. Please,...."

There were some details and then the bang.

The team took Maryann's car and left me with the jalopy. I called Chief Harkon from the mobile home and administered what first aid I could to old Carl wearing his underpants, whose face had been redecorated for no reason. The drugs he was on kept his pain down and his memory in tatters. His girlfriend's brains were spattered on the kitchen wall. There wasn't anything I could do for her.

Steve took his brass with him this time.

ELEVEN

The festivities wanted only alcohol to set things in motion when we pulled up to the picnic pavilion late in the steamy but otherwise dry afternoon. I had napped for an hour and shaved for this without enthusiasm. I kept hoping we'd be rained out. No such luck. The sun was determined to spite me.

Klem and Wringer argued over the tap they were misthreading into a keg. I remembered Wringer's last operation and the secret little award we gave him for coming home alive. He and Klem were swearing at each other with plenty of vehemence.

I decided they were not my quarry. Both were too low on the totem pole to be bothered by Steve.

Maryann put her casserole dish on a picnic table. It lined up behind chips and dip, a bean salad, three potato salads, and a relish tray. The next table held bags of hamburger and hot dog buns, bottles of ketchup and mustard, pickles, mayonnaise, and sweet relish, bowls of sliced tomatoes, lettuce leaves, and chopped onions. Napkins, paper plates and cups, and plastic spoons, forks, and knives covered the third table. A space had been reserved for the large trays of burgers and hot dogs that would come off the grill when things got going.

In the meantime, Klem shoved Wringer into the table, scattering plastic utensils over the cement floor of the pavilion. Wringer's wife helped him pick up the plasticware and put it back neatly on the table, then pushed him toward the tap.

"Hurry up," she said. "I want a beer."

Theresa brought another contribution from our house, and for the first time, I noticed what she was wearing. I disapproved entirely. It wasn't just the tight fit of her shorts, but the little top she wore did not quite meet the shorts' waistband.

It shouldn't matter, I thought. They're back at the safehouse sifting information. They won't dare show up here. The last thing they need is for a bunch of babysitters to be able to identify them.

Of course, like the sun, they showed up.

I could feel The Brat's eyes on Theresa's bare midriff. He was sitting with the others in the armored black Mercedes I had acquired for them. The one with properly mounted radios and a working car phone. The one with tinted windows that maintained their security in the face of all the faces staring at them from the pavilion.

The entire Section was there with their families. Charlemagne was not blown, the Section was. Everybody knew the legend. They knew who was in the car. I scanned the paled faces of my subordinates. One man almost wrenched his wife's shoulder out of its socket as he shoved her behind him to hide her. I wondered which one of these people wanted Steve dead.

Then Steve got out of the car. Announcements don't get any clearer than that. Whoever commissioned the hit on Steve now knew he was up against Charlemagne. Things would get desperate from here on out.

Steve held the passenger door for me and climbed in the back seat with Louis and Charlie. We proceeded to sit there, facing a subdued holiday picnic, while I named every man sweating in the humidity under that pavilion. No doubt Steve had already done the honors, but for some reason, I was required to do the same again. And they didn't even need bamboo shoots to make me do it. I was gauging the likelihood of each person being the quarry even as I pointed him out. It was this that Mack was reading on my face.

"So, six," he said. "You suspect six of your men. And The Woman?"

He said it with the capitals, the way it is said in The Section. Steve must have told him how to pronounce it.

"She would be a strong seventh," I said. "But she's still in the Amazon. I spoke to her this morning via satellite. I have the coordinates so I know she's there, and the satellite link is the only communication she has. Also, I don't think it's her style. If anything, she would seduce Steve, not kill him."

There were chuckles from the back seat.

"Let us go back to your house to discuss the list," said Mack.

"Why my house?" My voice was pretty sharp.

"We are hungry. The food you provided is terrible."

"I didn't provide it. Whoever you pressed into service on this—I'm presuming it's Turner—is still doing the catering. All I did was get you this car."

"Go, tell Maryann to come home."

"And to bring back the food she brought here," said Charlie.

Louis hissed. He is such a food snob.

I walked up to the pavilion and was accosted by so many agents, I could not find Maryann.

"I thought Steve quit," said Sturgeon. His fishy brother Cod nodded.

"Why is he riding with Charlemagne?" asked Barcode.

"Maybe he got a new car," I said as I scanned the crowd.

"He got out of the passenger side."

"Maybe it's a British car," said Mole.

"Maybe you're a dumbfuck," said Skosh.

"Are they supposed to be in the country without a babysitter now that Bear quit?" said Beauregard, always a stickler for the rules.

Mole said tsk tsk and it sounded like a twitter.

I spied my wife and daughter talking to a group of women in front of a table laden with salads. The men who were not mobbing me had clustered around newly arrived coolers of beer.

I fought my way through the crowd and told Maryann to pack up and meet me at the van.

"We should leave the food," she said, "It's far too much for us."

"No. All of it."

I looked around at everybody in earshot. Luckily, the initial crowd of senior officers was busy arguing and would not hear me. The juniors would not be as adept at understanding that I meant to feed an army.

Maryann opened her mouth to argue.

"Just do as I say," I said heatedly. She gaped at me. I don't think I have ever addressed her in that way. Theresa stared wide-eyed.

"Give me something to carry," I said, more as a way to cover the moment for the sake of the entire audience.

There was stony silence as we loaded my wife's pink car and Maryann drove us out of the park.

"I'm sorry," I said.

"They're coming over, aren't they?"

I stared at her with new appreciation. "You should have been an intelligence officer."

"I have seven children. Of course, I can figure out something that simple."

Theresa piped up from the back seat. "They're coming over? Charlie too?" The voice was way too eager for my taste.

Maryann gave me a sideways glance. "Honey," she said to the rear-view mirror, "I think it would be best if you do not encourage Charlie. Your father doesn't think it's a good idea, and I think he's right."

"But why?"

"He's too old for you right now, for one thing," said Maryann.

"But that's not why Daddy doesn't like him."

My women were better intelligence operatives than my crew. I took a deep breath and let it out with a hiss.

"Tell me, sweetheart," I said, "when you kiss him, do you put your arms around his neck?"

"Ye-es."

"Do me a favor when you kiss him today," I said, avoiding a sharp look from my wife. "Put your arms around his waist and slide your right hand up his side, under his arm."

"Dad! I know he wears a gun like you do. It's not going to shock me."

"No, just listen. When he stops you, look in his eyes. That's all I ask. Don't be playful; don't keep trying, just look in his eyes. Okay?"

Maryann's jaw was so tight, her lips turned white.

"If you say so, Dad." I couldn't see it, but I could hear her roll her eyes.

The Mercedes was there when we pulled up. They were already inside. Sally and Steve were having a public discussion on the front lawn for the entertainment of the neighbors.

TWELVE

In the general chaos of my household, with the food, the dishes, the noise, the jackets taken off, ties loosened, the sulking of Sally, and seething anger in Steve, I wanted a quick breath of peace in the chair next to the piano in the living room. It was already occupied by the Frenchman. He raised an eyebrow. I guessed it was too much for him, too.

I had forgotten my instruction to Theresa, so when Junior, son of battering ram, hit me square in the gut and pushed me up against the wall next to the sofa, I heard Steve's voice as I tried to breathe, and became vaguely aware of a growing audience.

"What the fuck did you say to her, old man?" said Charlie as he tightened my tie for me.

It is impossible to speak without breath.

"Daddy, I'm sorry! He asked me if you told me to put my hand there. Charlie stop it! That's my dad!"

He loosened his grip and I found sufficient breath to say, "I only told her to look in your eyes when you stopped her. You told her the rest."

This got me the response I expected. What I didn't expect were his words as I struggled again for air.

"Did you tell her about you, Frank? About what you did?"

"Frank?" murmured my daughter.

"Your father," said Charlie. "His game name is Frank. Has he told you? Did you tell her, Frank? I was there, you know. I watched them die that day, you fucking bureaucrat. Don't act like you're better than I."

"Than me," I wheezed. I couldn't help it.

"That is not grammatical," he said.

"It's not if the word 'than' is a conjunction, but it is grammatical if it's used as a preposition and that's what everybody says. Even educated people. It would make you noticeable."

There was a long, silent pause. Being noticeable is a sin. The only sound was my wheezing. The explanation had been expensive in air but paid for itself in time to breathe.

The Frenchman reached his hand over the piano and hit a few keys, just a noise, not even musical, then beckoned to Charlie. The young man took a deep breath, sat down on the bench, and played my favorite, Rachmaninov's second piano concerto.

Louis forced everyone into the dining room where we all listened while the music crescendoed, developed, progressed, and resolved before he and Mack made it clear to Maryann, Sally, and Theresa this was business they were not expected to stay for.

Charlie came in and took a seat at the table next to Steve. Mack opened proceedings.

"We think we know the origin of some of the money," he said. "But first, I want from you a brief description of your six subordinates. Tell us why you suspect them. Tell us also why you do not."

I wanted coffee. I wanted ibuprofen. I needed Maryann. I started with the fish brothers.

"Sturgeon and Cod went through training together," I said. "Sturgeon got his nickname because of his long pointy nose, and Cod because of his wide mouth. Sturgeon is from Wisconsin, Cod from Maine. I can't assign them to operations near each other unless it is a joint project relevant to their teams because they are constantly in each other's business. They socialize together; their families practically live in each other's houses. I suspect them because they whine continually about how unfair everything is. I think if it is someone in The Section, the most plausible motive, aside from some sort of sleeper mole, is jealousy about Steve's promotion. I think these two resented it.

"I don't suspect them because neither one of them would have wanted the job. It would mean breaking up their collaboration or even their friendship. They are comfortable with the status quo. I don't think they would want to change it."

I really needed coffee. I needed comfort, maybe some arnica for my bruised ribs.

"Who is Mole?" prompted Louis.

"He is the quintessential moaner," I said. "I don't suspect him of being a mole. His nickname comes from a character in a cartoon. He looks just like him. Pointy head, no neck, beady eyes. He objected to the name at first, but now he takes it in good part because he doesn't have a choice. He even keeps a fez on his desk as part of the joke."

I received a generalized blank stare all around.

Steve explained, "The cartoon character wears a fez."

Some cultural nuances just cannot be sufficiently conveyed.

"Mole is another one who did not take Steve's promotion well," I said. "He was number two after The Woman. I could not pass her up, though, and just give it to the next man, so I gave it to the last man in The Section and Mole let me know how deeply he disapproved. He also made Steve's life a living hell when he got back from Chicago."

Steve nodded his agreement with this.

"I could exonerate him based on sheer cowardice," I said. "He would never risk his worthless neck, or lack of one, by taking on a team like this. Do you think we can get some coffee?"

Mack sent a pointed glance Steve's way.

For somebody who had spent most of his time at the bottom of the pecking order, Steve was slow to catch on to his more important duties. Mack put an elbow on the table, supported his forehead with his hand, and glared at Steve from under his palm.

Steve left the room and we all sat in silence until he sat down again.

I resumed with the next name on my list. "Barcode got his name because of his pinstriped suits."

The door opened to Maryann and the blessed coffee, except there wasn't any. She came in bearing only the burden of a worried look. Mack stood because Maryann, a woman who was at least technically not a servant, had entered the room. The rest of us stood because Mack did. Steve and I were not used to this. Nor was Maryann.

"There is an African American man at the door saying he is with the FBI," she whispered in my ear.

"ID?"

"Yes, he showed me one, but I don't know how their IDs should look."

"Did you let him in?"

"Of course not. Not with them here," she said through her teeth, using just her eyes to indicate whom she meant.

We were all still standing. I'm pretty sure it was not sitting well with Mack.

"Jay Turner is here," I said. "He's outside. Do you want him invited in?"

Jay was none too pleased about being left waiting on the front step, but what really bothered him was what he had to announce to Mack.

"Your safehouse is under surveillance. I have to move you. "

What really bothered me was what he said next.

"It occurs to me you should just stay here. It is a big house, apparently unsuspected, and Cardova has a secure line."

"Who is Cardova?" asked Maryann.

Jay turned to look at her. "And I'm told the food is better."

"The house is not big enough," I said.

"We could ask the boys to stay at the coach's house," said Maryann, "but Theresa's best friend is out of town this week, so she can't go over there."

"If the boys are already out of the house," said Jay, "let them stay out, but don't evacuate anybody. It will call attention to the place." He gestured at the team. "You need to stay out of sight and we will have to do something about the signature Mercedes, which is why I did not provide one in the first place. We must also retrieve your gear."

Steve and Charlie brought the Mercedes back later that night after fetching all the gear and backed it into one side of my garage. Jay Turner provided two teams of watchers to dry-clean their route. Maryann gave Jay a grocery list.

By eight o'clock Sunday morning, the second day of my vacation, I had the houseguests from hell, and Maryann was making pancakes.

THIRTEEN

Theresa passed the maple syrup to The Brat with a smile. It was not the wished-for troubled smile of revulsion and horror. That look was reserved for me.

In the next instant, I forgot my worries about my daughter because my wife was giggling and blushing over something the Frenchman had said to her as she put a platter of sausages and biscuits on the table. She was wearing makeup and looking considerably un-pudgy, and judging by where his eyes were, the Frenchman was appreciating that fact.

The Brat took it all in and grinned at me with malicious enjoyment as I lost my appetite and bit my tongue so hard I could taste blood.

Sally sat on my left, with the highchair to her left and back a bit, then Steve next to her, and Louis to his left, next to Maryann. To my right was Mack, and then his son. Theresa sat down between Charlie and Jay on Maryann's left. I almost caused a scene about it, but Maryann gave me a warning look.

"The more you object," she had said that morning as we dressed, "the worse it will be for you. Even aside from all the physical contests you have no business joining, you now owe us, Theresa and me, an explanation about what Charlie mentioned. You do know that, don't you?"

The memory of my nonresponse to her prodding made me gaze into my coffee, the only thing in that noisy, chaotic room for which I had any appetite. Mack interrupted my reverie of self-pity.

"We must discuss the operation. You need to know about the money," he said.

"Not in German," I said. "My wife speaks German." Not that anything we said at this end of the table would break through the distraction of whatever Louis was saying to her.

"French?" said Mack.

"Frank's French is abominable," said Louis.

"I'll just listen, then," I said with some heat. "I'm really good at listening."

There was a silence, like the kind that inhabits disaster. Even Sally and the toddler paused in mid-argument over the throwing of sausages.

"Hey, pass me the butter, will you please?" Jay asked Steve, and the moment passed.

Louis and I did not exchange gunfire.

Mack began to brief me. "The money may have come from China, or rather, a Chinese source here in the US, since it was all well-used small denomination dollars. We have a description of the contact."

"How did you get all that?" I said, impressed.

"Charlie and Steve visited the man the courier named Brasser. His contact was a short Asian man who did not speak English well."

"When did you do this?" I asked Steve. "And where is Brasser now?"

"Last night before we retrieved the gear," he said as his face hardened. "He met with an accident."

"Your French is worse than your German," Louis told him.

"If that is possible," said Mack.

Sally threw down her napkin, yanked the child out of his chair, and left the room. Maybe she speaks a bit of French, I thought. I made a mental note to find out the languages of everybody's wife in The Section.

"It's been almost twelve hours," I said, looking at my watch. "Should I be calling Chief Harkon?" I had him on speed dial now. "Did you pick up your brass?" I asked Steve.

"No brass," he said. "His neck broke."

"He fell down the stairs," said Charlie. "It was a quiet apartment building. Gunfire would have been too disturbing."

I saw Theresa blanche just a bit at this baldly cold statement from the man she liked kissing, and I remembered vaguely that she had taken French classes in high school. Surely she did not know enough of the language to understand this conversation, did she? I made a mental note to find out all the languages of all the family members of all the members of The Section, and to start with my own.

Jay Turner had no language aside from English, to my knowledge, and blithely allowed Maryann to heap the last of the pancakes and bacon onto his plate.

I had eaten nothing, and my coffee was cold.

The meeting droned on as meetings do. There were too many inputs, too many asides, and too many questions. The Frenchman told too many risqué jokes while ogling Maryann's backside as she cleared the table. Once again, I forgot I was hungry.

Mack brought me back to the meeting by banging his palm on the massively expensive table I had grudgingly bought after Maryann's sustained campaign for it some years before.

"We are discussing your subordinate," said Mack when he had my attention, "the man you call Skosh. He is on your list." We were back to English for Jay's sake.

"He's Japanese-American, fourth generation." Then in response to several blank stares from around the room, I added, "You said the contact was Chinese. They're not the same, you know." My understanding of European geography far outstrips my knowledge of Asia, but I do know a few basics.

"Skosh is on my list because I'm pretty sure he could kill a man," I continued. "I kind of doubt he'd hire anybody to do it for him, though. I did not select him for the promotion because I need him too badly in the Far East. His expertise is considerable."

"Presumably his contacts are also considerable," said Jay.

"True, but he is pretty contemptuous of all non-Japanese Asians. I can't see him getting cozy with the Chinese. He disagreed with my selection of Steve because he thought it was stupid. The reason I have serious doubts about him being the one is that he thinks most things we do are stupid. He spreads his contempt around liberally and without prejudice. I don't think he cares enough about Steve to kill him. And finally, the contact was a short Asian man. Skosh is quite tall, thus the nickname. It means short."

"I should meet him at his dojo," said Steve. "His sensei is a Ryukyuan from Okinawa."

Theresa came in with a fresh pot of coffee and laid it on the sideboard.

"Do you think that's wise?" Jay asked Steve.

Steve shrugged. "He's a black belt. The best way to know a man is to fight him."

"My mom says the best way to know a man is to kiss him," said Theresa, smiling at The Brat to my right. He grinned back.

If I was ever meant to have a stroke, that was the time. I half rose from my seat, flung out my arm, and pointed at the door. "Out!" I shouted with everything in me and then some. Theresa was truly horrified now. She stalked out with the obligatory slamming door as commentary.

It was the first time in years she had obeyed me.

Mack shortened the momentary thrill of victory. "Your daughter is of age," he said quietly. "It is her choice, and my son will not hurt her. I worry that you will make yourself ill. Or worse."

I had a hot reply ready on my lips when my brain engaged with the subtle, ambiguous threat in the last two words that is his hallmark. My lips closed tightly and I swallowed into oblivion something along the lines of 'spoken like the father of a son' before I remembered why he had no daughter and the role I had played in that.

It was the first time I had ever been grateful for one of his peculiar threats.

FOURTEEN

"It occurs to me," said Jay Turner, "that the words 'or worse' may have been a threat."

"Ya think?" said Steve.

He was in the back and Jay rode in the passenger seat of my wife's pink car. I was driving us to Steve's afternoon appointment at Skosh's dojo.

"That's the thing with Mack," I said. "You're never really sure if the words are a threat because they can mean different things, but you are sure you feel threatened."

"What do you think he's threatening you with?" asked Jay.

"I think he plans to cut my throat."

There was silence all around until Jay said, slowly, "Maybe. But I think if he intended that, he would have done it by now."

"I agree," said Steve. "He doesn't waste time between decision and execution." There was another pause at the last unfortunate word, given the topic.

"While death is certainly bad compared to making yourself ill," Steve continued, "there is something worse than both in Mack's book."

"What?"

"Fucking up the operation. I think he's worried you're irrational about Charlie and Theresa and will blow up at the worst possible time."

We rode in silence for the next ten minutes, while I rehearsed a long internal speech I wanted to make about how it is not irrational to want someone other than a killer, even an extremely well-paid specialist, for one's daughter, even if it's just a kiss, and no amount of assurance that he won't hurt her means anything when he's armed to the teeth and I know for certain his intentions are way more than a kiss. We pulled up to the dojo. The plan was for me to stay with the car while they went in.

Before Steve closed the door, he said, "If it makes you feel better, Charlie didn't take out Brasser. He was just winding you up."

I had already checked with Harkon. Brasser's neck was indeed broken. I had thought in the next few days Steve would be either dead or fully operational. Hell, he had just told me he was already fully operational. It didn't make me feel better.

Steve did not look even winded when he threw his holdall in the back thirty minutes later, pushed it over, and sat next to it. Jay climbed in front.

"It's not Skosh," said Steve.

"He was very respectful of Steve," said Jay.

Shit. Skosh knows. "Did you beat him?" I asked Steve.

"Yes, of course."

"And?"

"And he's a really good fighter, but he uses only one style. I surprised him with a move I learned in high school wrestling. Took him down, and that was that."

I swallowed hard, not wanting to ask. Steve glared at me in the rearview mirror.

"For fuck's sake, Frank, we left him very much alive."

"And as I said, very much more respectful," said Jay.

"Something you might want to try, Turner," said Steve.

One arrogant smart aleck in my house was not enough. Charlie had a clone. I pulled Steve aside before we went inside.

"Tell Mack I will behave," I said. "I won't fuck it up."

Maryann handed me an ice-cold dirty martini as I came through the kitchen door. I took a sip and kissed her on the lips. She blushed for me, which I found delightful until I saw the Frenchman sitting behind the kitchen table cleaning a submachine gun.

"We need to talk," said Maryann.

"Yes, yes of course. After I sit down a while."

"You really need to talk to Theresa."

"I will. I will." I escaped to the living room and sat in my favorite chair, pretending this was the end of the second day of a fabulous vacation. Jay joined me, sitting in the matching chair before the fireplace. He also had a martini in his hand. I calculated how long my good vermouth might be expected to last.

"Why aren't you in Chicago?" I asked between sips.

"I saw the traffic come in about Five-Fifths, so I took a few vacation days and came down to see what was up. Took the opportunity to give the local office chief a break. I owe her."

"You alerted Charlemagne?"

"Yes."

I'd like to say we sipped our martinis companionably, but the truth is the atmosphere was tense.

"And brought them into the country? Yes of course you did," I said, answering my own question.

"Look, Frank. I know you believe in the established order and the rule of law, but your very job takes place in the cracks where there is no order and there are no rules."

"I believe in method and procedure," I said. "With authority and oversight so that the cracks, as you call them, don't swallow us unawares. I opt for civilization, my friend. I don't want the denizens of chaos invading my comfortable life. That is why I do this job, to keep them at bay."

Not to invite them into my home with my wife and my daughter. I didn't say it out loud, but Jay knew very well what I meant.

"You know, Frank," said Jay, "my people have rarely fared well under the established order."

"And yet here you are, one of its officers."

"I am," he agreed. "Insofar as that order protects the weak from the strong, I am a card-carrying member. When it fails or reverses the protection, I intervene. I like to think I saved Sally and the baby. I don't give a damn about Steve, but his son did not shoot down that airliner."

"And the woman courier?"

"She was not just a courier," said Jay. "She was a key part of the Five-Fifths US network, she and Brasser. That, at least, is part of my official remit, to keep outside networks off US soil."

"But not by acting as judge and jury," I said.

"Come on, Frank, what jury is going to understand the evidence, even if your bosses ever consented to release the information?"

I wanted a second martini, and so did Jay, but Mack called another blasted meeting and both of us were too professional to walk into the dining room sucking on olives and holding martinis in our hands. There was a pot of fresh coffee on the sideboard. I poured myself a cup as a consolation prize.

"Frank," said Mack, "tell your women we must not be disturbed."

Like that was going to go over well.

It did not go over well.

FIFTEEN

I have to admit that as meetings go, those run by Mack are above average in purpose and relevance. Sometimes he lets people get too creative, like when they discuss scenarios and responses, but on the whole, he makes them stick to the point.

This meeting was about Steve's assessment of Skosh as an enemy. Short answer, in Steve's words, "It's not him."

"Why?" said Mack.

"If he wanted to kill me, he would do it himself. He wouldn't hire somebody. He would not use Chinese money to pay them. His family has been here for four generations but is still very Japanese. They spent the war in an internment camp. They have, or at least he has, a kind of special arrogance against the Chinese. And given the history between the two countries, I don't see them dealing gladly with someone so culturally Japanese."

Mack got an entire cogent paragraph out of Steve with a one-word question. When I asked him a question, the answer was usually a grunt.

"There are two more men on your list," Mack said to me. "Tell us about them."

Of course, I had no business discussing my agents with a foreign specialist in the presence of his entire team, but I had learned some home truths about loyalty and the established order less than a year before and I was committed to this operation in a personal way, completely outside official channels. I had no moral framework like Jay's on which to hang this decision. I was doing it because I felt bad for Mack, for Steve, and even for Charlie. I did not feel bad for Louis, who shared equally in the present danger. I especially did not feel bad for him when he was flirting with my wife.

I cleared my throat and launched a detailed discussion of Barcode and Beauregard.

"Barcode is one of my favorite subordinates and would have made a perfect babysitter for Charlemagne. I did not choose him because without him, we would have lost his team, who are not in your class but are first-rate nonetheless. I don't know if Barcode resented being passed over, but I would have resented it. He lives alone and seems to exist only for the job, is a lifelong bachelor, and practices the most perfect tradecraft I have ever seen. He would be largely undetectable if he were to have a plan to kill Steve. That fact and his pinstripes, which earned him his nickname and are an abomination of the highest order, make me suspect him, but his long unblemished record tends to clear him."

I took a deep breath before describing my least favorite subordinate.

"There is not a lot to say about Beauregard except that he irritates me. Always and in every instance. Beauregard is from the bayous of lower Alabama, just above the Florida panhandle. The self-appointed arbiter of righteousness in The Section, he finds fault with absolutely everything. He is on my list for two reasons. He seems to find more fault than usual in Steve, and he disapproves of Charlemagne. I don't know why. He is not cleared to see any WEDGE material; he has never been briefed on any Charlemagne operation, and to my knowledge Steve has never discussed the team. I know I have not."

Steve said, "He wanted to give me the benefit of his wisdom when I got back from Chicago. I tried to be tactful, but I think he was offended when I wouldn't discuss the op or the team."

"Does he discuss other teams with their babysitters?" asked Charlie. "Or did he single you out?"

Steve considered the question. "It's not just me. He gets into everybody's business, always trying to be avuncular about it."

"Does he succeed?" asked Louis.

Note to self: conduct a briefing about not discussing teams even within The Section. Of course, the answer to Louis's question was yes. Steve did not blab much because he was suspicious by nature and not popular among his peers. He also preferred a workout in a martial arts gym to having a beer with the guys, giving them another reason to distrust him.

"Does either of them, Barcode or Beauregard, have an Asian connection?" asked Mack, just as Maryann came in. He did not stand.

"Please don't mind me," she said. "I'm just going about my duties, fulfilling my womanly role serving coffee." She placed a fresh pot on the sideboard and noticed me shaking my head. "Don't you shake your head at me, Leo. We will discuss this later."

I rolled my eyes. "I was just answering Mack's question, not shaking my head at you. Thank you for the coffee, now...."

"You're wrong, Leo."

"Huh?" Sometimes words evade me. I expected a continuation of the sniping I had experienced earlier when I told her to stay out. Note how she obeyed me.

"You're wrong," she said. "They both have connections."

All the eyes that had been trying to stay out of a marital tiff were now on my wife. When the silence lasted more than a beat, Maryann said, "I'm sorry. I should not have spoken. Silent and obedient, that's me." She picked up the empty pot.

Mack sighed. "Tell us."

"Me?" She put the pot back down and stood with her hands on her hips. "It's not like I have anything to contribute other than food and drink, serving wench, and kitchen drudge that I am."

There was a guffaw from Louis. Mack gritted his teeth and said, "Please."

Mind you, she knew how dangerous he was and did not care. She was that angry. But she answered him. "Barcode's dad was a flamethrower at the Battle of Iwo Jima. He was seventeen. Imagine giving a seventeen-year-old marine a flame-throwing machine or whatever they call it. He attended a couple of our get-togethers and told me he still has demons from the war and not a lot of love for Japan. Not surprising, if you ask me."

She was speaking to a man who cuts throats for a living. But he's not seventeen. Nor do I think he ever was.

When she did not continue, he prompted her, "And Beauregard?"

"His wife's uncle, or great uncle…," Maryann thought for a moment. "She's too young, a bit of a gold digger if you ask me. Beauregard must have been almost twice her age when they married, so it must be her great uncle."

Mack so perfectly controlled his impatience that he was more still than usual.

"His wife's great uncle, then," she continued, "was Claire Chenault's crew chief. They go to Flying Tigers functions every once in a while. She told me there is always great Chinese food at these dinners, and presumably Chinese people as well."

The last words were a bit pointed as was her semi-glare in Mack's direction, and she concluded with, "Dinner will be ready in half an hour and I will need to set this table. If that is all, m'lord, I'll be going about me duties."

She actually curtsied before picking up the empty pot and sweeping out of the room.

The Frenchman exploded with laughter and pounded the table. Jay Turner and Steve shook silently. The Brat grinned at his father, who allowed a half smile to show on his face.

"She is magnificent!" said Louis, pointing at me. "If you do not reward her tonight, I will."

Given what I knew of the Frenchman, I was sure when I was alone with Maryann later, that I had no choice.

SIXTEEN

Before I could reward my most excellent wife, I had to get through another meal with a houseful of unwanted guests. Jay went missing temporarily. His place was set, but if he did not get back soon, he would starve. Maryann had made roast beef with all the trimmings, and most of us were on our second plates when Jay finally showed up.

Maryann tried to wave him into his seat, but he stood in the doorway with a worried look, wondering how to proceed with so many in the room. The longer he hesitated, the quieter the room became until even the baby stopped squawking.

Mack looked up and put his knife and fork down. "What is it?"

Jay drew in a deep breath. "There is another team in town."

"Who?"

"Potemkin Village."

This was an up-and-coming Eastern European team that could someday rival Charlemagne. Someday soon. They often worked for the Soviets but were essentially freelance and specialized in deception schemes. Their explosives expert was considered one of the best now that Sobieski was dead.

Mack shrugged one shoulder and waved to Jay's seat. "Come. Eat," he said, ever the gracious host in my own house. He did allow me to retain my seat at the head of my table and deliberately ignored my pointed stare.

The conversation changed with Jay's announcement. Mack began another meeting, right there among the mashed potatoes and gravy, and in English. He was rude and arrogant at the best of times, but tonight he opted for just arrogant.

"We will go to the sovereign house in this city," he said.

It's actually outside the city, because parking is a problem inside, leaving the half-mile restriction on violence around a sovereign house meaningless when there is no place to park within the limit. Also, when things are too congested, our city streets restrict the possibilities of safe ingress and egress by making ambush too easy. The concept of having a refreshment stand, so to speak, where warring factions could meet in safety was too important to forego in a city where every warring faction in the world showed up regularly, so someone had the bright idea to invade an old clubhouse at a golf course on the outskirts. It was called Chucky's because the concept itself wasn't already scary enough. Occasionally, a clueless politician showed up there to play golf and was escorted politely off the premises.

"When?" asked Louis.

"Tonight."

"Who?" This from Charlie.

"All of us."

Louis wiped his lips on his napkin and sat back in his chair. He looked at me. "We will need a babysitter."

"We will need both," said Mack.

"I am not a babysitter," said Jay.

"I'm not going anywhere," said Sally as she wiped little Danny's hands. "I don't need a babysitter."

Steve put his hands over his face. "I've told you repeatedly what a babysitter is, Sally," he said through his fingers.

"You men and your silly games. It's time you got a real job, Dan." She took the baby out of his highchair and walked out the door.

There was a stunned pause at this strange mixture of delusion and willful ignorance. Maryann raised her eyebrows. Even my daughter opened her eyes wide.

Mack tore his gaze from the retreating Sally and looked at Jay. "You are the domestic authority here. Our presence must seem officially sanctioned. Frank cannot conduct an operation on American soil."

I wondered if the son of a bitch knew my highly classified job description as well as every other fact of my life. Of course, he did, I concluded with a sigh.

Mack addressed me, having read my mind. "Your laws about internal surveillance are public, and your personnel policies are easily obtainable with Louis's skill." Was there a hint of a smile? *I need to take up Zen to empty my mind of all thoughts.*

He then favored me with an unmistakable smile. I shivered. "I've never gone into a sovereign house with you," I said. I did not want to start now.

"You must be there publicly, in the car, so they see we are here officially. Also, you will park your car behind the Mercedes. There are no sensors on the car, and Todor Chilikov is very good with plastique. You should take the FBI car, not the pink one."

"Who will stay here...?" Charlie swallowed the words 'with the women'. Wise boy.

"Can't I come with you?" Theresa asked Charlie.

"No!" Even Maryann joined in that chorus.

"I can add another team of watchers outside," said Jay.

"Someone should be inside." Again, Charlie avoided saying, 'with the women.'

"What about Skosh?" suggested Steve. "He can fight and he doesn't miss much."

I had my misgivings about Skosh, but the man had taken defeat with dignity and Steve did have fleeting moments of good judgment, provided the subject was not female.

"Skosh and Maryann will defend the house very well," said Louis, smiling at my wife. She smiled back.

...

Armed and arrogant as usual, Skosh arrived in good time. Maryann was by my side at the front door. Sally and Theresa came into the hall a moment later.

"Is this some weird job interview or something?" Skosh asked me. "Because if it is, I'm not interested. My team's the best in Asia and that's where I want to stay. I don't know anything about any other continent and I'm content with that."

Before I could answer him, the team walked in, wearing suits, having shaved and combed their hair. By the team, I mean all of them because Steve was obviously part of it. He had the look, the alert gaze, and the tight jaw. I heard Skosh whisper, "Shit," and I knew Steve's judgment was right once again.

Before we left, Mack pointed at Theresa and Sally. "You," he said, "will obey Maryann and Skosh exactly, in all that they say. Am I clear?"

Theresa gulped and nodded.

Sally stood defiant, glaring at him.

One moment, he was standing a few feet away. The next, he was directly before her, his knife in his hand, the blade before her face so that she looked at the edge cross-eyed. Though I had seen its results many times, I had never seen the actual instrument before, never in almost twenty years. For the life of me, I did not see him deploy it. It seemed too large to have come down his sleeve, but maybe that was a trick of a dangerous moment. It moved again so that the tip was under her chin, lifting it so her eyes were locked on his.

"This," he said, "is my game piece in the silly games men play. If you disobey those two at all, in any way, I will use it to gut you like a fish. Now, am I clear?"

"Yes," she whispered through her teeth because she did not dare move her jaw.

The knife disappeared, again seemingly without movement. Mack looked at Skosh and said, "Do not let her out of your sight. Theresa and Maryann will look after the child."

"Yes, Sir."

They walked through the kitchen and out the side door to the Mercedes in the garage. Steve did not look at his wife.

I passed Skosh on my way to the front door. "Fuck, Frank," he said. "In your own house?"

I walked down to the street to join Jay in the FBI car and saw at least one pair of his watchers a few yards away.

"Why are we doing this?" asked Jay.

"They need intelligence."

"About Potemkin Village?"

I nodded. "I think Mack suspects this is less about Steve and more about Charlemagne."

"A trap?"

"Precisely."

SEVENTEEN

We sat in Jay's car watching the Mercedes before us until the gunfire began and we were tempted to run and see. We kept our eyes glued on the Mercedes.

"What do you suppose?" said Jay.

"I suppose they put up some wannabe thug to attempt a distraction for us to leave the car."

"I was thinking the same. Why don't they just shoot us?"

"Because first, that would alert Charlemagne that the car is insecure and second, we're inside the half-mile perimeter, just barely, but inside. Bad form."

"Not bad form for the thug?"

"No. He doesn't, or rather, didn't know the rules."

"Didn't?"

"When he was alive."

"Did Charlemagne kill him then?"

"Charlemagne or any number of others. The rules are enforced by the clientele. I'll have to wait by the body for Chief Harkon. You'll need to follow them back to the house. Do you have watchers standing by to help with the dry cleaning?"

"Three teams."

"Excellent. Here they come."

I noticed the blood right away, and the wheezing peculiar to a man in pain. Steve staggered for one step and Louis steadied him.

"Whose bullet?" I was asking about the bullet that killed the shooter, whose identity was no longer important. I knew he would be dead.

"Louis's," said Mack.

I nodded. "Jay will cover your back as you get to the house. I called Chief Harkon on Jay's car phone and will wait by the body. Where is it?"

He pointed, told me the distance, and after the briefest nod, climbed into the Mercedes.

Harkon raised an eyebrow at me, but that was all. "Who shoots such a weak charge?"

"Someone who is very, very accurate."

"Evidently." The chief looked at the small hole perfectly placed between the man's eyebrows. "You're never going to explain all this, are you?" he asked, shaking his head. "No, no, of course not. Shit. I thought I had a dirty job." He patted me on the shoulder as I took my leave.

I took a taxi and was only a few minutes behind by the time they had insured themselves against a tail. At home, I walked into a world war with venue in my living room.

Everybody was there: Jay and Skosh hiding in a shadowed corner of the room, Theresa watching fascinated, the team standing with stone faces, except Steve, who was leaning on Louis and bleeding on my carpet, and Sally in full throat about the hardships of her life, all of it directed at her fading husband, the sole author of her troubles.

"That man threatened me and you did nothing!" she screamed, pointing at Mack. "He's dangerous! That one, your best friend," her arm swung to Charlie, "is the son of Satan! And the other one is just a clown."

The clown was wearing his most dangerous smile. I am sure if he'd been able to let go of Steve, he would have shown her just how funny he could be.

Sally's diatribe continued into a downward spiral of incoherence but an upward one of volume, when Maryann came out of the kitchen, her arms covered in flour. She faced Sally squarely, drew one flour-encrusted hand back as far as she could, and let fly a mighty open-handed slap across Sally's face.

"Get a grip, Sally!" she said. "You listen to me. Your husband is bleeding on my living room carpet and your son is upstairs screaming for his mama. Pick one and go to his aid. We'll take care of the other one."

When Sally ran upstairs sobbing, Maryann turned to Louis and said, "What do you need?"

Louis respectfully asked for boiled water and the use of the dining room table. Politely even.

Everybody bundled into the dining room, where we laid Steve out on my expensive table and watched as Louis removed his holster and shirt. The holster, or rather, the Smith

& Wesson in it, had saved his life. The bullet that would have killed him shattered the gun and traveled a little way through the leather of the holster, cracking a rib and leaving a shallow dent in his chest. It forced a piece of the firing pin into his upper chest just below the shoulder, breaking a minor vein, causing stains on my carpet, and not inconsiderable pain to Steve.

Charlie brought the medical bag in from the Mercedes parked in the garage. Theresa followed with a large bowl of boiled water and a stack of clean tea towels.

"Mom went upstairs. She said to tell you there is a shaker of martinis in the fridge," she said, with an obvious intention to watch while Louis dug out the shrapnel and sewed up the wound.

Skosh took his leave with a wince, as Louis brought out a scalpel.

Mack and I also took the hint and found the shaker. I retrieved a jar of olives from the back of the bottom shelf where I had hidden it, and we made ourselves comfortable at the kitchen table.

"Have you told your wife?" asked Mack.

"No."

"You must."

"I know." I took a large sip of my martini.

"Why am I still alive?" I said. I figured I might as well ask it since we were already on this excruciatingly painful subject.

Mack considered me a moment. "At first," he said, "I thought you would be more useful to us alive. As you can see, I was correct. Then, I learned you had become more thoughtful about your blind obedience to a flawed system. Perhaps you did not deserve death."

"I have never been blind to the flaws of the system," I said.

"Yes, I am aware you and Jay discuss such things interminably. You are Ismene to his Antigone."

He must have had a bug in Jay's car.

Mack continued. "I am locked in a prison bounded by monsters, but most people in this civilized world are at the ordinary fleeting mercy of petty bureaucrats and do not know it." He sipped his martini, savoring the taste of my excellent vermouth, and resumed. "I know what I am and do not pretend to any morality. But there is power in small decisions, and we think nothing of the destruction they cause."

"There is a wide spectrum of guilt," I said, feeling mine acutely.

"Between me killing one man with a knife and another man killing millions with a pen? That is a wide spectrum, but the difference between two discreet instances can be very small. The holocaust depended on the many who thought they were doing their duty, like Eichmann. He was proud of his work."

"Still," I said, "even flawed order is necessary or the need to survive makes killers of us all. It is a paradox."

"When you arrive at the paradox where order meets chaos," said Mack "you only begin to understand the question."

"I believe in the necessity of order," I said, "and yet I acknowledge my guilt within it."

Mack raised his eyebrows and finished his martini. "So do I. And because I did not kill you when you deserved it, the Mercedes did not blow us up tonight. We are alive to drink martinis and discuss the nature of paradox."

...

I climbed the stairs strangely comforted by what I thought might have been a compliment from Mack regarding my steadfast guard over that Mercedes in the face of gunshots and general emergency. I mulled over his words and thought I could make a good case on the compliment side of things, as opposed to the threat side, which was more usual.

As I came near Theresa's door, I was surprised to see Louis come out of her room. He raised an eyebrow at me, lifted his bag of sensors as an explanation, and entered the next room, presumably to install perimeter sensors outside the window there as well. Despite the obvious explanation, the encounter made me uncomfortable enough to knock on her door. She answered me from inside. I asked if everything was all right. She assured me it was.

As I walked away, I heard her giggle and stopped to listen, but there was no further sound. I hesitated in the hallway, reviewing everybody's whereabouts. Jay was downstairs taking the first babysitter watch. Mack was on watch for Charlemagne, wearing a headset plugged into a radio receiver designed to monitor the sensors, supposedly more reliably than the green screen. Steve was sleeping off a low dose of painkillers on the sofa next to him. Louis had not come out of the next room. Sally and little Danny had gone to bed long ago and anyway, Theresa had no use for the woman. Maryann was waiting for me in our bedroom.

My foot stepped forward, drawn in the latter direction, then back in indecision. If I went to Theresa's room and she was alone, had giggled perhaps at something funny she was reading, she would be angry and at a time when I owed her at least my trust. If I went in and she was not alone.... because of course the only one unaccounted for was the son of Satan himself. I had given my word to behave myself, but I knew I would not, could not, because although Mack was right, she was an adult, she was also my last baby, the darling of my life, and I would act without thought and without care and either get myself killed or destroy the op or both. And the op, this unofficial, non-sanctioned op born out of chaos, held my wife and daughter as hostages.

I had an inkling, the merest shadow, of life locked in a prison bounded by monsters.

I continued to my room, where Maryann was waiting.

EIGHTEEN

I spelled Jay a few hours later and spent my watch drinking warmed-over stale coffee with the Frenchman in the living room. Steve surfaced, sore and still groggy, but demanding coffee of any description other than weak.

We were all in the kitchen an hour later that Labor Day morning, the beginning of my third day of vacation, trying to figure out how to brew more coffee, when Maryann and Theresa came in with smiles like Cheshire cats. Maryann's smile gratified me until I saw Louis's sly grin, but Theresa's reminded me about last night, who had been missing, and what I wanted to do about it, when she put her hand on my arm, taking the coffee pot from me and giving it to her mother.

"Dad," she said, "I'm the last in my class to give it up, and the only one to give it so well, to an exciting man I will remember forever. So, I want you to be sensible about this."

If she thought that was supposed to help, she was wrong. I prepared a moon launch, beginning with my blood pressure.

"He did not hurt me, Dad. I will still start college when this is over. I'm not going anywhere, still living here, and I'm not marrying anybody. It was my decision."

Maryann gave me a maddeningly compassionate smile. Louis had the grace to leave the room. Steve stayed, though. He was a born intelligence officer who also needed coffee.

"Louis knows I speak French," said Theresa.

"I didn't know you speak French."

"He read my high school transcripts," she continued. "He placed a sensor outside the window while Charlie sited his rifle, just in case, he said. Have you seen his rifle, Dad?"

I've seen what a sniper rifle like that does to a human body. But I said nothing.

"Then Louis left, and well, Charlie followed his instruction about being gentle." Theresa was doing her best not to laugh out loud, her face adorably full of dimples.

Now I wanted to kill Louis as well.

By the time Mack came in, I had my first cup of decent, hot coffee in my hand and felt more in control of myself. I knew eventually Steve would give Mack the entire story in execrable German. I swallowed hard. It was the first time I was the knowing subject, not the recipient, of prime intelligence. Mack raised an eyebrow and I knew that he knew that I knew…. You get the idea.

…

I had just sat down to a plate of scrambled eggs and bacon in the company of the usual crowd seated at the dining room table—which Steve had bled all over the night before—when Jay waltzed, no stomped in, addressed me, and said, "Come on. We gotta go."

Quite apart from his use of gotta instead of his usual 'must needs', Jay's manner told me this was urgent. I looked at my plate in sorrow.

Jay would have stomped out the same way, but Mack raised his hand.

"Sorry," said Jay. "Here." He shoved a shopping bag across the table at Steve.

Then he turned and tried to head off the man coming through the door. Chief Harkon stood in the dining room and surveyed the scene. Because he was visibly armed and unexpected, the response was immediate. The Chief was covered by three handguns pointing lethally at head and heart. It would have been four, but Steve had just begun to unpack his new Beretta.

"I told you to stay outside," Jay said through his teeth.

The Chief nodded slightly at Mack and lifted his hands into the air. How did he know this would be the one to worry about?

"Come on you guys," I said. "He's a cop."

Mack gave me a withering look, then lifted his chin at Louis, who was closest. He relieved the Chief of his sidearm and patted him down. Turnabout is fair play, I suppose. He found a small pistol strapped to Harkon's ankle. There was also a wicked-looking knife in his belt, which Louis slid across my flawless dining room table to Mack, who put away his SIG Sauer.

I saw Harkon turn pale as he watched Mack open and weigh the knife. I offered him the seat between Mack and Charlie. He declined.

"What is it?" said Mack to Jay.

"One of Frank's guys is dead," said Jay.

"Which?"

"Everybody's here," I said, puzzled.

"No. One of your guys, one of your spooks," said the Chief. "I called the FBI when I knew, and the ballistics match the gun of another one."

"Who?" said everybody ever born, including those at my breakfast table.

"Doyle. The dead guy, that is. Or was," said Jay.

"Barcode?" I asked. "And the match?"

"Steve Donovan. His Smith & Wesson."

"That file is on a secure computer. And the S&W is in pieces on my living room coffee table. When did Barcode die?"

"Last night at about ten," said Harkon.

"I know, I know," said Jay. "Ten o'clock is when Steve was shot. It gets even better. A bullet from a gun registered to the dead guy who shot Steve near the sovereign house was embedded in the door jamb at Barcode's apartment. Registered, mind you, and with the ballistics on file."

"Two-bit thugs don't usually register their guns," I said. "So there was a woolly plan to stage a shoot-out scenario between Steve and Barcode? Did you secure the premises?"

Harkon nodded.

"I expect we'll find something that incriminates Barcode regarding the Chinese," I told Jay.

"This is very crude. It cannot be Potemkin," said Mack, still playing with the knife.

"No. It's not them," I agreed. "It's someone in The Section who wants to get away with killing Steve but is too stupid to know when to quit. You can give back the Chief's weapons. We're leaving."

I had managed to scarf half my plate during the discussion, grabbed the remaining bacon, and ate it on my way to Jay's car. The Chief followed us with no other comment but a low whistle and climbed carefully into his squad car.

Harkon got there before us, having the benefit of lights and siren. Barcode had lived in a third-floor walk-up efficiency apartment. The place was spartan in the extreme, so I wondered how our quarry would have managed to plant the evidence so as to be credibly hidden but still easy to find.

"Those guys in your dining room, Leo," he said as I walked by him. "Are they houseguests, or something?"

"That's about the size of it, Chief."

"Or something," said Jay under his breath.

"And your guy who died here?"

"He wasn't involved. He's an innocent bystander."

"I'd hate to see what happens to the guilty among y'all."

"Yes, yes you would hate to see it," said Jay, under his breath again, but perfectly audible.

"Oh, I saw a bit back in that warehouse the other day," said the Chief. "Six of them, and one of them, who must have been a lookout, had his throat cut." He made a slicing gesture across his neck.

Now I remembered and realized why Steve had vomited in the car. He had been there at the time.

Jay found it; a tiny book full of daily cipher keys tucked almost, but not quite, carefully into the bottom of the phone on Barcode's bedside table. Conveniently, there were no signs of any actual messages. We were supposed to believe he deciphered messages at home and then did what with them? Burned them on a hot plate? Ate them like in a bad spy movie?

I was looking for an idiot. An idiot who had called in the deadliest of Charlemagne's current list of enemies with the help of at least one foreign power, after a failed attempt at killing a colleague with the help of a different foreign power. Steve might be my guy's target, but he wasn't Potemkin's. He and his family were now the bait.

NINETEEN

"You are usually more timely in your perceptions," said Mack.

I was back at my dining room table, empty of food, both me and the table. Mack started the meeting with this assessment of my realization that Charlemagne was now the true target.

I could tell Steve's reaction to my observation was a wisely unspoken, ya think? I was prepared to take him down a peg, new gun or not. He had disassembled his new Beretta 92SB and laid the pieces on the bare wood of the table, along with an oily cleaning rag and a leaking bottle of solvent. I took a coaster out of a drawer in the sideboard and slid it down the table at him. He looked at it, puzzled.

"For the solvent," I said.

His puzzlement continued until Louis leaned over, picked up the solvent, and put it on the coaster.

It already had etched a small ring into the finish.

We were all tired, of course, on day three of an op that was as opaque as it had been on day one. Two bystanders were dead, and both for no good reason. One had been duped into certain death. The other died as a too-obvious red herring. We had clues and suspicions, but no hard facts.

Mack did not look pleased, and he was looking at me.

"I have gone over the entire Section roster," I said. "The remaining five of the original six are still the most likely by a mile. I should say the remaining four. Skosh acquitted himself well and I think we can use him again. That leaves Beauregard, Mole, Cod, and Sturgeon. All of my initial impressions hold. Beauregard remains my least favorite person, which is why I distrust my preference for him as the culprit."

"This house is still secure," said Jay. "There are unknown watchers on the safehouse and some freelance watchers on the Donovan house, but nothing here."

"For the moment," said Mack, "we are as secure as we can expect to be in the circumstances. Potemkin's attack is likely to be by explosives. It is their strength. Where is the pink minivan? Can we pull it in alongside the Mercedes? It should remain unknown."

"Done," said Jay. And he made it happen. Good man.

We went back to first principles and decided Potemkin's main attacks would consist of deception and explosives.

"The entire op has been deceptive," said Charlie. "Are the Chinese even involved?"

"I think they are," I said, "or were, but only because they were given an opportunity to suborn one of my guys. They now have him by the short and curlies and are not likely to let go. He has to be getting uncomfortable about it."

"Short and curlies?"

I opened my mouth to answer, but Theresa came in with more coffee. Louis explained, en Français, which I knew he knew damn well she spoke. I glowered at him. He grinned. She blushed. So did Charlie, to his credit.

"I want the personnel files of all four men," said Mack.

"I can't...."

His stare hardened.

"No, listen," I said. "I'm not refusing. I'm officially on vacation and can't go into the office to get any files without calling attention to it."

My relief at this easy excuse was short-lived.

"Then we will retrieve the information and you will tell us how."

His voice was soft as butter and sharp as his knife. He wanted me to compromise the entire Section. The room was silent. Everybody understood. Even Theresa, who was holding hands with The Brat.

"If it helps you," said Louis, "we have most of it already, as do the Soviets."

So many thoughts and arguments went through me. Did I trust them? Of course, I did. I trusted them to look after their interests entirely. Did I have a choice? Maybe a slim one. But this was not the time to add even a small resentment to the mountain of seething fury that sat within this relationship. What made me decide? The word 'Soviets.' I looked at Louis when I said, "Fine."

Of course, I would change all the codes and safe combinations the moment they were done and have the place thoroughly swept for devices.

Of course, they knew that.

But what Louis knew about what the Soviets knew was my quid pro quo, and Louis knew that, too.

I made it clear to Theresa that she should leave. She resisted until Charlie gained the cooperation from her that I could not.

I told them in which office down which hallway they would find the records. There was a pause.

"Is there a computer in the vault?" asked Louis.

First of all, he shouldn't know about the vault. Second, the vault had nothing to do with the original request for four personnel records held in a file cabinet safe in a different room. Third, the computer... *Shit.* The computer.

I just kept telling myself 'Soviets', over and over, as I gave the cipher lock codes, the alarm codes, the combo to the file safe, the combo to the walk-in vault, and finally, the passwords on the computer.

I was now thoroughly compromised, not to a foreign power, but to a team of foreign freelance killers I had known for close to twenty years and to whom I owed an enormous debt of guilt. I hoped it was now paid by this abject surrender to necessity but knew better. I had made only a down payment.

This is how it is done, I reflected, the trade in information. It was my bread and butter and I was swallowing a relatively mild poison with this meal, in comparison to some. So which of my four agents had been exposed in this way to Potemkin Village? We never used that team. They were primarily a KGB asset. Which of my guys would even get close?

TWENTY

"**W**here the fuck is your car, Frank?" said Steve. "We need it tonight. We can't take the Mercedes. Misha asked me and I had to admit I didn't know. I hate fucking having to admit things like that to Misha."

After my initial irritation at this rich change of deference toward his new boss now that it was no longer me, I noticed the name he was using regularly now for Mack, and the irritable tone typical of an exposed specialist during an operation. How would Sally deal with this transformation? She had not dealt well with the husband of three days ago. What would she do with this new one? Would she understand what had happened? Would she even believe it?

Maryann drove me to the shop for my car in the pink minivan.

"Leo," she said as we pulled out of the driveway, "are we in danger?"

"Yes," I said after a moment's thought. She was never easy to fool, so I did not bother to try.

"Equally? I thought it was just Sally and the baby."

"Not equally, but all of us."

"Because of those men or from them?"

"Both. Again, not equally. The outside danger is far more potent and is directed at Steve and his family and the team itself."

"And those men staying with us," she said, "what do you call them?"

"Charlemagne. It is the name of their team."

"You've known them for some time?"

"Nearly twenty years. I first met them when they were around Charlie's age."

She was quiet while she negotiated a left-hand turn across traffic. As we pulled into the auto repair shop, she said, "Would that man be capable of gutting Sally like a fish?"

She placed the minivan in park and set the brake before I replied.

"I've never known Mack to make a threat he was not prepared to carry out," I said carefully. "He doesn't bluff."

"Oh, Leo." She turned to look at me. "All these years, this is your job? Every time you went away?"

"Yes."

"I've been so comfortable all this time," she said, looking away. As I reached for the door handle, she said, "But I still want to know what they want you to tell me."

My pause was momentary before I made a quick egress. "I know. I will."

Back at my happy home, with my car in the driveway and a pair of Jay's watchers keeping an eye, or rather four eyes on it, I walked into another world war between the usual combatants, Steve and Sally.

"I want to go home! This is stupid! There is nobody trying to kill us. The only threat to me came from that horrible man with the knife and you did nothing! He has a screw loose!"

"You're the one with the loose screw, Sally. Why won't you listen to anybody? Why did it take a knife, his knife, to make you shut the fuck up?"

"You're just playing your silly games, acting all macho instead of getting a decent job and providing for your family!"

There was more, much more, all of it variations on a theme of why can't you be more normal?

Steve's answers were less varied and boiled down to why can't you shut the fuck up about it? He was under massive pressure, still in some pain, and had not slept more than four hours in the last twenty-four. The look he gave her as Maryann pulled her into the kitchen told me a year might be too generous an estimate of their chances.

Mack, Louis, and Charlie had not been in the living room as this went on. I wondered where they were. Probably rifling through my study, I thought, as Steve walked back to join them. When the three of us came into the kitchen, I closed the living room door just in case, because I was about to impart a few home truths and did not need an audience. Maryann began making lunch, and the steam soon over- whelmed our inadequate fan system, so I opened the door into the dining room, checked it, and was satisfied it was de- serted. The blinds were drawn, but the extra air was wel- come in the hot kitchen.

Sally blubbered at the kitchen table, nursing a cup of tea, no doubt provided by Maryann, but I noticed there were no 'there theres' coming from that quarter. Maryann was as fed up as I was. It is fine to be concerned for the safety of a fel- low human being, but it becomes increasingly difficult when the beneficiary of our concern is a ninny, which is the word I knew Maryann would use to describe Sally. I had other words. She was a beautiful young woman. I knew very well what Steve was thinking when he married her. But she would never be a Maryann when they were our age. If they lived that long.

I sat down across from her. "Look, Sally," I said gently but as firmly as I could, "Steve has a job. He has been hired by the number one team of freelance killers in the Western world. I can't put it any plainer than that.

"He lives in a world where everything is vicious and deadly except you and Danny. He is a hunter and is hunted and is himself becoming vicious and deadly. That is never going to change. He will only get better at it. And his name is now Steve. I'm sure he told you that, many times. When you refuse to acknowledge the name change, you endanger him, yourself, and your son even more. Do you understand?"

She shook her head.

I sighed. "At least try to take in what I am telling you. Steve is never going to be normal. He will never hold a middle management salaried job. He will never mow the lawn in a suburban yard on Saturday and play golf on Sunday. He will fight and get badly injured and go do it again as soon as he's healed, even as you saw him last night with the shrapnel in his chest. No doubt, he will die young."

She picked up her head at this and said, "If he dies, can I go home?"

This chilled me more than anything I had ever heard out of Mack. It was a completely unthinking, cold menace that is impossible to counteract. I prayed the Frenchman did not have a listening device in the kitchen. I knew Mack already had no use for the continued existence of this empty-headed woman. That she could be so callous and selfish about the life of a team member, her own husband, would make her life forfeit if he found out.

"Sally," I said through clenched teeth, "every time you cause trouble with the team, and I repeat, Steve is on the team, you threaten me and my family as well. Does that fact register with you at all? Because it is very much front and center with me."

She gave me a scornful look. "This is all nonsense. I don't have to listen to this anymore and I won't."

I got up from my chair so as to have some leverage to shout at her. My arm was ready to point and my mouth open when I saw a long, slim leg, expensively clad in summer-weight grey wool, stretched out on the left side of the door leading into the dimly lit dining room. I closed and opened my eyes. Maryann gave me a questioning look, then saw the leg, then paled. She stood by the counter facing the open doorway.

I went through the door and turned to face them. The Frenchman sat now on my right, Mack on the left, in chairs on either side of the door. Both were in shirt sleeves and shoulder holsters, their weapons gleaming in the dimness. The Frenchman spoke.

"We found something on your computer."

I had pegged it. They had been in my study.

"We came to tell you, but the conversation," he gestured toward the kitchen, "was interesting, so we did not want to disturb you."

Mack leaned forward, resting his forearms on his knees with his hands clasped before him, and looked up at me. "Can we be heard in the kitchen?"

Maryann nodded.

"Yes," I said.

"Vasily enjoyed American women," said Mack. "He said they did not seem to know danger. His American wife understood the most subtle threats, however." He raised his eyebrows. "She still does. She heeds them. This one does neither. She is a danger to us."

He was perfectly still, staring a hole through me with laser-blue eyes. I knew the last sentence to be the deadliest I had ever heard him say. He normally employed only one solution to people who endangered the team.

"I will kill her, but not today. It would not be good for Steve. But she remains a threat."

He sighed and stood up, walking with that incredible stillness into the kitchen where he addressed Maryann. "Your reward nights with your husband must wait. He will have duties elsewhere anyway. I want you to be in this woman's presence at all times." He pointed to Sally. "She is to sleep with you. You will accompany her to the toilet. If she does anything other than care for her ordinary needs or those of her son—Steve's son—you must alert one of the team."

He spoke then to Sally. "Do you understand this instruction?"

She rolled her eyes. "Like that's going to happen."

"If you do not understand my words, perhaps you will understand this."

He crossed the room with that strange still movement of his, yanked her by the arm out from behind the kitchen table like an explosion, and backhanded her face, hard, sending her flying into the refrigerator door. Maryann stepped away from the counter and out of his way because he was already standing over Sally as she gasped for breath and in the next instant lifting her and backhanding her again so that she fell into the chairs at the table.

"I'll call the police," she gasped.

"Do you think you will live until they arrive?"

He looked at Maryann. "Do not leave her."

"Yes, Sir."

I had never seen him hit a woman. I had seen him kill a couple. I mean I saw the results after the fact, but they were enemy killers trying to do the same to him. To my knowledge, he had never hurt a non-operational woman, at least not personally. Threaten with an intention to fulfill it? Plenty. Show pity when the operation went that way and an innocent death was unavoidable, no. All of this I had seen, but I did not think he would strike a non-operational woman. He stalked out of the kitchen.

I had also never heard my wife say 'yes, sir' to anyone. She gave Sally a pack of frozen peas for her eye and a tea towel to wrap it in.

Louis came in looking for coffee. Maryann handed him a cup, shaking. He put his arm around her shoulder. "It is okay, *mon cher*," he said. "No one will hurt you."

"I teased him," she said. "I defied his edict to stay out of the meeting."

"And you were right to do so. You provided valuable intelligence. You have nothing to fear."

"He was so angry just now."

"Angry? Non. He is desperate. We do not know what to do. He had to make her believe his threats. Frank tried reason. She is impervious to both, so Misha tried to show her. She should be killed or otherwise neutralized completely, but we cannot because of the child."

Louis sighed. "No, Misha is not angry. This was a calculated move, like everything he does. I am the one who can be emotional and destructive. I would have killed her long ago."

Maryann registered the businesslike tone, for want of a better word, and opened her eyes wide at the man who had kissed her hand. She turned back to the pan beginning to sizzle on the stovetop.

"I'm going to sue that bastard," Sally said. She sat on the floor in a corner of the cabinets, holding the peas against her eye.

"I think sometimes it is not a good thing to feel too safe," said Louis, smiling wryly at my wife. To Sally, he said, "It is important to remember that men are dangerous, Madame. *Vraiment,* all men are dangerous, but some are deadly."

"Now do you understand why I do not want Theresa anywhere near Charlie?" I said in a low voice.

"Ah, it is too late now, *n'est-ce pas?*" he said. "Theresa is not like Sally. She knows Charlie is dangerous. It is because he is dangerous that she likes him. You have much to learn about women, my friend. I wonder how it is you won your excellent wife. Maryann liked the danger in me also." He grimaced. Maryann did not look up from the pan sizzling on the stove, but I could sense her tension. "Until Misha showed her what such danger can mean." He sighed again.

Louis left the kitchen shaking his head as Sally muttered about lawyers from her corner.

I sat at the table, elbows propped, with my head in my hands.

Maryann made lunch in silence.

TWENTY-ONE

L unch was not festive. Not subdued either. More like funereal.

We took our usual places. No one dictated where we should sit, but we repeated the pattern we had established at the first meal as happy families do in any house. Maryann and I sat as hostess and host, she near the kitchen door and I across from her. She was subdued. If Sally had received an intravenous infusion of threat medicine from Mack to almost no avail, Maryann overdosed on the fumes. I could see Louis on her right doing his best, but her smiles at him were half-hearted. I found myself regretting it as much as he did.

Five people at the table did not know about the kitchen education session: Jay, Charlie, Steve, Theresa, and Danny the toddler. All of them, without exception, felt its aftermath. Danny was so good, nobody noticed him in the highchair, and he ate all his peas.

Steve, of course, noticed the shiner on his wife's right eye, and the bruise on her left cheek. I saw the questioning glance he sent to Mack, who was as cool as a glacier and gave nothing away.

I was concerned when Sally glared at Mack in defiance. I knew about prisoners who use defiance with their interrogators even while under torture, but those brave people do so with full appreciation of the danger they are in. Sally had no such understanding. She defied a man she considered a liar and a game player, despite the contrary evidence of the pain in her eye. I saw no courage in this, only folly.

Steve noticed the look, of course. It added to the question on his face caused by the sight of her injuries. She put more peas in the bowl before her son. To everyone's surprise, except that of his parents, one oblivious to her danger, the other distracted by it, Danny again ate them dutifully.

"That man hit me," Sally said to her husband, indicating Mack across the table from her.

The table was utterly, completely, fully, profoundly silent. No one breathed. I swear it. I know I didn't breathe.

There was a long eye-to-eye, right across my nose almost, since they were close to me, Mack to my right, Steve to the left, one seat and a highchair down. Steve's query exchanged with Mack's glacier.

"Sally," said Steve softly and kindly, as he began the happy families approved method of uncomfortable public family fights no one wanted any part of. "Your life and Danny's life depend on your cooperation. Can you see that? When I got back from Chicago, you understood it. What happened?"

"Our future depends on you coming to your senses, Dan. You should have stayed in the Air Force. You were going to be a general one day and you had to go and give it up for no reason and now you have this stupid job with the frog man and these nasty people and that man hit me!"

Nobody ate. Chewing would cause noise.

"I was never going to be a general," said Steve. "It was never in my nature to toe the line that well for that long."

"But you went to the Academy. Daddy said those people become generals. I was raised to be a general's wife."

"Most of us never become generals, Sally. Jay over there was much more distinguished than I was, and he is not a general."

Jay did not seem to appreciate the attention. He dropped his eyes onto his plate.

"Of course not," said Sally. "He's not as handsome as you are. If you can't be a general, then you should get a good job so we can buy a nice house and Danny can go to a good school. I'm not unreasonable, Dan."

"We've talked about this, Sally. I have the best job I can get and we have to move or people will come and kill us."

"I'm not listening to this nonsense anymore. I'm going home. I will not be made a prisoner in this awful house!"

She stood up and tried to take Danny out of his high-chair. Steve stopped her. She turned on her heel and moved behind me heading for the door at the other end of the table that led to the living room. Mack was in her way. He leaned back in his seat and, almost casually, grabbed her arm as she tried to sweep past him.

"Let go!"

He said nothing.

"I need the bathroom."

"Maryann has been working all morning and has not finished eating. You must wait for her," said Mack.

I noticed Maryann put her napkin beside her plate and open her mouth to say it was quite all right, but Louis put his hand on her arm and gave the slightest shake of his head. She subsided and picked up her fork, though like everybody else, she did not eat.

"This is so stupid! You can't make that old woman my jailer!"

I could feel the disapproval in the air. Maryann was universally esteemed. Of all her provocations, this disrespect of my wife was the thing that lost Sally the most sympathy from everyone in the room. The Mack-induced bruise and shiner were forgotten, even by Theresa.

"Sit down." His voice was at its most menacing softness.

"Make me."

He obliged.

She sniffed and looked at her husband from her usual seat at the table.

"You make this necessary, Sally," said Steve.

His manner was as glacial as his boss's. He picked up his fork and ate, as did Mack, now back in his seat. Everybody, except Sally, had lunch. I don't know what her expression was as she sat there. I kept my eyes on my plate.

Danny ate more peas.

TWENTY-TWO

I was helping Theresa clear the table after lunch when Mack came back into the dining room and with the barest sideways movement of his head, summoned me. Theresa saw the summons and took the stack of plates from me.

Mack turned and walked toward my study. I followed, as I plainly was expected to do. Once in the room, he sat in my chair at my desk, which disturbed me not a little. Louis sat on a corner of the desk. The younger men of the team sat in chairs that had been brought in from the back patio. There was a third chair empty. Mack pointed to it. I sat.

Why am I here? I thought with alarm. This was a team meeting, with listeners unwelcome in the extreme, held in my study and chaired by Mack sitting at my desk. I did a mental inventory of everything that might be in the desk drawers, the small filing cabinet, or the credenza behind the chair which held the secure phone and the home computer. I'm pretty careful as a rule, but complacency can create egregious lapses. I have been guilty of that from time to time, usually whenever fate calls for maximum damage out of minimal mistakes.

"You are here," said Mack, reading my thoughts as usual, "because we will be discussing matters that concern you."

Technically, every op concerned me. It was my job. But he meant the word concern in a slightly different context that suggested something personal, the very worst connotation of the word. I was duly concerned.

Mack pointed at me with an open palm. "If you write any of this down, Frank, I will slice your carotid and require Theresa and Maryann to watch you bleed out."

I swallowed hard. "I give my word."

I figure there is a difference between recording privately and securely for one's own memory and writing for file. This will never be in any file. And it's not written.

Nonetheless, I swallowed hard again, especially at the way he indicated my family by naming the ones present in the house. A piercing look from those blue eyes made me swallow hard a third time.

He looked at the others. "Do you see that? He gives a reasonable response to a known threat!"

"You are not a monster, Papa," said Charlie.

Steve and I exchanged a quick look regarding the irony here. Slapping a woman rated the monster scale, but other, um, things didn't?

"Then why does it feel otherwise?"

Louis answered, with an acerbic tone. "Because Alex will disapprove."

Tension and warning bounced around the room with an accompanying pause to allow everybody to keep his temper or prepare to intervene as the case might be.

I presumed Alex disapproved of a lot of things. She was also very familiar with what Charlemagne did, not just for a living, but to continue living. She had been naive once upon a time, but never a fool and was disabused of her naiveté early on. Would slapping a particularly obtuse woman who threatened everybody's security qualify one as a monster while threatening, with obvious sincerity of purpose, to gut her like a fish did not? These were heavy questions and I was glad Steve still saw them as such. I could see them going through his mind. I suspected he would soon lose the faculty of recognizing such ironies.

I also knew in that instant that trouble was brewing in Charlemagne. The Frenchman's sharp jibe and Mack's razor-thin answering look suggested a rift. The name Alex indicated the reason. The unspoken communication I saw between Charlie and Steve confirmed why Charlie was desperate to have him on the team. I felt smug about my deduction for about a nanosecond before Charlie saw it on my face and afforded me a silent and additional virulent threat to his father's of a moment ago with just an ice-blue stare. I was swallowing hard a lot lately.

Mack returned to the business at hand. He directed a discussion of Potemkin Village.

"Jay says they're still watching the safehouse," said Steve, "or somebody is, but now not as heavily as they are my house. He says they have hired or otherwise acquired an army of watchers and a few rent-a-thugs, all of them concentrating on my house. The Potemkin team itself is probably based within the neighborhood. There are quite a few houses for rent nearby so it wouldn't be difficult."

"Why?" asked Louis. "Do they think you will go back there with a woman and child, alone? If so, why the army?"

"They do not expect him to be alone," said Mack. "We have announced he is one of us. The army is for us."

"But so obvious? What is their plan?" asked Charlie.

"They hope for an unexpected event to draw us," said Mack. "which brings us to the mole in Frank's office. There are too many suspects, too many clues, and none seem applicable to anything." He pushed his hair back from his forehead and looked at me from under his fingers.

This was my moment, it seemed, and I had nothing. Desperation called a few things to my mind and I practiced a little out loud brainstorming with them.

"I still think the mole, at least, is after Steve and it's personal," I said. "He must be a bit of a coward, especially since Steve is tough to beat in any fight, so he had to seek funding for a contract. Also, maybe he needed help making arrangements outside our normal channels." I paused, feeling my way through this line. "The Chinese took him up on his offer first but bowed out when it went sour and they lost an entire team. Ever the opportunists, the Soviets acquired the option and decided to exercise it, using Potemkin Village, which is known to have its own agenda regarding Charlemagne. My mole did not set out to compromise himself. He just wanted rid of Steve. But he's probably desperate now. Compromise is easy to acquire and impossible to escape."

I knew this last bit of wisdom too well.

"Which brings us to another reason why you are here, Frank," said Mack.

Was he rubbing it in? I had begun to think I had given my two cents and would be dismissed to repair to the kitchen and be rewarded with a martini, but Mack thought differently.

"If we live through this operation," he said, "we will take Steve and his family with us. Once your mole knows they are gone, he will come for you. He will learn that you and your family harbored us and Steve. He will want your family as well. He has shown he has no ordinary scruples by targeting Sally and the child. Maryann and Theresa will never be safe. You will enter the black without skills and without resources."

I was absolutely speechless because he was absolutely right.

"When we find the mole," he continued. "it is essential we receive a commission on him. You must not depend upon your orderly system to keep you safe. It need not be a large commission, but we must have it and execute it before we get on the airplane. Do you understand?"

I nodded dumbly.

"Can you acquire it within eighteen hours?"

I gave another dumb nod. I knew he wanted a proper commission as part of his quest to bring Steve into line, but he was wrapping me up tight in a straitjacket of obligation and implication that would last the rest of my life.

The other revelation in his last question was that he expected to be wrapping up the operation itself the next day. I had no idea how that could be; it was still such a woolly mess.

The meeting was not over; there was more to come and none of it involved a cold, dirty martini. Mack looked at Louis, who addressed me.

"Your computer is infected."

"My computer?"

"This." He indicated the home computer sitting on the credenza behind my desk.

I was becoming an expert at dumb nodding. He rolled his eyes. "I have traced it to this game." He held up a disk. "The virus collects everything you do on this computer and deposits the information on this disk."

"It's a good thing I don't do anything on the computer, then," I said, a little resentful of his condescending tone.

"Maryann uses it for recipes and Christmas letters. The kids play games on it. I never touch it."

"Yes. This is a game. One or more of your children must play it. The information stored here began to be gathered just before we came."

I nodded, not quite as dumb for a change. "If it's a shooting space game, it belongs to the boys, otherwise it's Theresa's. She likes those word puzzle games."

Louis nodded at Charlie.

"I will speak to her," said The Brat.

"You will not!" I snapped. "I will."

"Charlie will," pronounced the judge sitting behind my desk.

I seethed as the topic changed.

TWENTY-THREE

"Steve," said Mack, "I am afraid that until Sally decides where she will stay and under what terms, we cannot allow her to know anything about Vasily's Carpet. We will instruct the pilots to land at night and will blindfold her on the approach to the house. Alex will arrange rooms for you, Sally, and Danny within Vasily's Carpet, but Sally will not be permitted to leave those rooms until you and she can negotiate a reasonable solution. As she is now, she is a grave risk to us, and we cannot allow her to know anything at all."

By this point, I had replaced seething with being as still as any fly on a wall can be, praying nobody with a fly swatter would notice me. This was detailed inside information.

"I don't get it," Charlie said to Steve. "When we were at your house while you were on your way to Chicago last year, all we did was open our jackets and let her see the weapons. She understood right away. She was tight-lipped about it, and nervous, as she should be, but she understood and did as instructed. What changed? What has unhinged her?"

Steve threw his head back and slumped in his chair, legs stretched before him. "I wish to God I knew."

Louis asked it. Of course, he would ask it. "She is beautiful. Do you make love to her frequently?"

Steve narrowed his eyes, rejected the possibility of not answering, and said, "She won't let me."

"How long?" said Mack.

Steve paused to remember. "Maybe a month."

"Someone new has come into her life then," said Louis. "A man?"

Again, an intensely thoughtful look wrinkled Steve's brow. "Noooo," he said, stretching the word and shaking his head slowly. "Not a man. She doesn't go anywhere except to coffee mornings with the Section wives, and she even quit going to those."

"When?" Mack and Louis said it together.

Steve opened his eyes. "About a month. And she's always on the phone." I could almost see the creaking machinery in his head creating steam as he searched his memory for facts he never before had any intention of paying attention to. "Linda!"

"Linda who?" This time I joined the Mack and Louis chorus.

"I don't know. I don't know any of the wives."

After all, what could be more inconsequential than a bunch of middle-class wives? To my shame, I didn't know any of them, either. I always left that to….

Three of us stood at the same time. Louis sat further back on the desk laughing. Mack said, "Sit down. We are not finished. When we are, I will ask her while Steve stays with Sally."

"Um," I said, expecting the fly swatter any second, "I think I should ask her."

Please don't make me explain why you are the last person who can expect a coherent answer from my wife right now.

Mack's eyes dropped fractionally then looked at me. "Very well," he said, "but I must be with you." He raised a hand to stop my interruption. "I must see her face and hear her voice as she answers. Maryann will cope with my presence if you are there."

"Tell us about Sally," Louis said to Steve, as serious as I have ever seen him.

"I met her in Colorado Springs during my senior year at the Zoo." He saw the question on our faces. "The Academy. I was in my last year. She was a waitress. She had a degree in something from Colorado State, but she was waiting tables when I met her. To tell the truth, I was pretty desperate to get in her pants, so I proposed. She accepted, and we had the big deal military wedding in the Academy chapel right after graduation. After that, pilot training at Reese in Lubbock and F-15 lead-in at Luke in Phoenix. She hated every minute of both. She spent a lot of that time at home with her parents in Colorado. Danny was born there."

"Then you went to Alaska?" prompted Louis. "Was she happy there?"

Steve closed his eyes momentarily. "No. She hated that, too."

I began to understand where the Frenchman was heading.

"Does Sally like to travel?" I asked.

"Fuck, no," said Steve. "The only thing she hates worse is moving. It took months each time just to unpack the boxes and by then we were packing again."

"So she doesn't dream of a romantic trip to, say, Venice?"

"Venice? You've got to be shitting me. You may as well suggest Mars."

Mack picked up the thread. "Has she ever traveled to Europe?"

"Hell no."

"Did you tell her you will be moving to Europe?"

Steve stared at Mack, pausing, swallowed, and said, "I told her yesterday."

Mack raised an interrogatory eyebrow.

"She went ballistic," said Steve. "She said Linda told her that would happen and that she would never see her family again and Danny would grow up talking in some strange language, and more like that."

"She fears change," said Louis.

"Yes."

"Her passport has no stamps on it?" asked Charlie, unable to believe the concept.

Steve's brow furrowed. "She doesn't have a passport."

I have to admit, I was part of the room-wide shock at such a concept. My kids had passports from birth.

"And the child?" asked Louis.

Steve shook his head.

Mack sent a very pointed look Charlie's way. "I'll have them delivered to the airplane," said Charlie.

"In eighteen hours?"

"In twenty. It will be that long before we can take off. What? They need not be authentic. They will not be required for US entry."

There followed a long-winded parental stream of criticism and blistering heat about Steve's irresponsible choice of such a wench, and now he had a son by her, his firstborn, and she would always be in his son's life and his, no matter what happened. Even if she were to die, his son would be damaged either by the association, the questions, or the lack of a mother.

After a while, I had the feeling that much of this speech was directed at Charlie. A glance in The Brat's direction gave me verification of the theory. He had the tight, sullen jaw and rolling eyes I have seen on Theresa's face any time I've tried to impart a few home truths.

I found myself reluctantly agreeing with every word Mack said and having no sympathy for the two blistered young men in the room. Louis was suppressing a chuckle.

I reflected that Mack did not like Sally at all. Not a good omen for Steve's marriage, but I was not sure Steve himself was all that invested anymore.

TWENTY-FOUR

We descended upon a peaceful kitchen like a murder of crows, dividing the women, taking Maryann and Theresa to other rooms, and neutralizing Sally's ability to overhear or even realize there was an interrogation going on, though little Danny provided all the cover anyone could want. He sent up a wail the minute Mack walked in the door. Steve held his son and Louis struck up a conversation about baby food with Sally.

Mack and I led Maryann to the study. On the way, I saw Charlie and Theresa sit down together on the living room sofa. Charlie held the computer game disk in his hand.

We sat in the three patio chairs still set up before my desk. Maryann glanced uneasily at Mack but was otherwise her usual composed self, maybe a little more on the somber side.

I considered my words carefully. I did not want the question to affect the answer.

"Maryann," I said, trying not to be the protective over-bearing husband I so wanted to be, "do you know if any of the women connected with The Section is named Linda?"

She furrowed her brow. "There are no women in The Section," she said, "except Millie and her name is, well, Millie."

"Women connected to the men, I mean, like mothers, sisters...."

"You mean wives. Why not just say that? Though there is one sister named Linda. She lives in LA. She came to dinner once with Barcode. He wore those awful suits, poor man. What was his real name? Del, Dale?"

"Doyle."

"That's it. She happened to be in town and agreed to even the numbers at a dinner party for me, but that was three years ago. He was a bit odd, I think, but it's a shame he died. Besides his sister, there are three wives named Linda."

"Which three, my dear?" I asked.

She named them. One was very junior. Another was support staff, and the third...?

"Bartok? Bertrand?" She was concentrating hard, too hard, on French names, I thought.

"Bertram!"

I did my best not to react. "Have you seen her with her husband?" I asked.

"Yes, of course."

I raised my eyebrows to urge her on.

"He's the one, you know, the one who looks like a bloodhound. They're from Alabama, I think. You call him...."

"Beauregard," I said to Mack.

I noticed he needed a shave and realized their usual sartorial precision had deserted them hours ago. Mack had rolled up his sleeves displaying forearms striped by scars. Circles under his eyes told me he was already functioning on adrenaline. We were getting close.

He leaned forward in the chair and asked Maryann, "Has Sally taken any calls from Linda Bertram?"

"I wouldn't know. I've only been her keeper since this morning."

My wife was becoming a bit more belligerent than I considered healthy under the circumstances, especially given the increasing stillness in Mack. Always a bad sign.

"You would know," he said. "You know everything that happens in this house. Has she?"

"Why? So you can hit her again?"

"As I recall, you also hit her."

"That was different. I had a good reason."

"What reason?"

"She was acting like a ninny."

"I hit her because she was becoming dangerous. Which is the better reason?"

"Don't fence words with me, mister."

"I dare not. But I must ask the same from you. I am the foreigner here. You have me at a disadvantage with your words."

"You're never at a disadvantage in anything, I would wager."

"I try not to be. What is your answer so that I may not need to hit Sally again?" said Mack, but with no smile.

"I don't believe violence ever solves anything," said Maryann.

"Yet your husband deals in violence every day."

"My husband is not violent."

"That is correct. He does not commit violence. We do that for him. Now, again, how do you answer me?"

"If I don't, will you hit me, too?"

"No. I will hit him." He pointed to me. "For failing to control his over-intelligent wife. Now answer my question."

The last sentence was an order, not a request, and I hoped she understood that.

"She has not had any calls."

"Did she make any?"

"Yes, but I don't know who she called."

Mack stood and held out his arm. "Come, I will return you to your duties as Sally's keeper."

I opened my mouth to protest, and he pointed at the secure phone on my credenza.

"You have something to do. How long before you will receive the authorization?"

"At least until morning," I said. "It's Labor Day. And there are only two very circumstantial proofs."

"There will be more before tomorrow." He pointed again at the phone.

A knock on the door interrupted us, followed by an impatient Charlie. "Bertram," he said.

"You now have three," said Mack.

I called my boss.

TWENTY-FIVE

Dinner was subdued. Two people were missing entirely. Louis and Steve had been sent to get some sleep. Jay popped in and out, grabbing what he could from the bread-basket, showing Mack various telex messages, and disappearing again. Charlie looked like he wanted to provoke something. Theresa was reading a book at the dinner table, a family mortal sin, but she had a dispensation from her mother. We all wanted to escape. No one begrudged her descent into innocent fantasy. At least it was more rational than Sally's mythology.

"So Sally," said Charlie. His father looked up sharply. "Tell me about Linda. Is she a fun person?"

"How do you know about Linda?"

"You mentioned her." Which was a lie. "Isn't she one of your friends?"

"She is. We laugh a lot, mostly about our sons."

"She has a son?" asked Charlie.

Theresa stopped reading and gave him a narrow look.

"She does," said Sally. "He's a lot older than Danny, of course, but still all boy. He knows about computers. I hope Danny will learn all that stuff. I'm hopeless with it. So is Linda. She's older than me, but we're very much alike."

"How old is her son?"

"Seventeen going on seventy, Linda says. He's always telling her about all kinds of dangerous things in the world."

"Does he? What about her husband? I'll bet he knows a lot about danger with the job he's in."

The Brat was a born interrogator. We heard a lot about Beauregard, his high opinion of himself, his low opinion of his colleagues, his family's strengths and shortcomings, and the sad state of the world. Mack was looking thoughtful.

"I only asked for the one," I said to him in a low voice.

"The woman may be a dupe," he said, "but the boy will cause you trouble later."

I think Charlie was campaigning for a package deal.

...

Acutely uncomfortable is how I would describe that night. Charlie had guard duty, you might call it, staying at my house with the women and assisted by occasional visits from Jay as he had time.

"My son knows better than to become distracted when he is responsible," said Mack. It did not make me feel better. I was driving my car with Mack up front and Louis and Steve in the back. They were going to burgle my office while Mack and I waited in the car. So many disaster scenarios ran through my brain that I ran up a curb while making a right-hand turn.

"Fuck, Frank," said Steve.

We drove to about half a mile away, let those two out, doused the lights, and crept up to just outside the perimeter sensors. Then we waited. The moon did its part by being new as opposed to full, but the facility was lit like daylight. Still, I did not see them go in. They were that good. Of course, they had the benefit of having extracted all my knowledge without having to torture me for it.

"So how do you figure tomorrow's the day?" I asked, making conversation.

"The FBI has intercepts from Potemkin and the embassy."

That no doubt they are not sharing with us. "That's right," I said, "Jay is your creature, isn't he?" I was a little piqued.

Mack turned his head to look at me. "You also are my creature, Frank."

Touché. Too-bloody-shay. "You did it very neatly," I said.

"I did nothing but accept the opportunity. Your guilt did most of the work."

"I said I was...."

"Sorry. Yes, yes. They are dead and you are sorry. And all your vaunted loyalty is plundering your computer system as we speak. Do you enjoy the irony?"

Why was his grasp of irony always so dark?

"You know damn well I'm not enjoying any of this."

I could feel him smiling and sought a change of topic. "Don't you think you were a little hard on Steve today? Did you know his parents died in a car crash during his third year at the Academy? Declines in both grades and behavior soon followed. That is one damaged young man."

"Of course, I know his history. If he does not learn judgment, especially with women, he will not live to be a damaged old man," said Mack. "My son was with them the day they died, Frank. Like Steve, he has very little family, a burning desire for vengeance, and damage. The two will be formidable by my age. If they live."

"As I recall," I said, "you were already formidable by their age. And damaged."

"Do you think anyone who does what we do is not damaged?"

Maryann had packed a thermos of coffee for me, with two mugs. How did she know? She did not know where we were going or why or for how long. She only knew we were an odd assortment at a weird hour of the night and in my heap of a car. Why not four mugs? Somehow, she knew it would be me and Mack.

To my surprise, he accepted the offer. We drank silently for a few minutes.

"You and Maryann have been married for thirty years."

"Yes."

"Longer than I have known you."

I nodded.

"Do you...?"

"Yes, we do."

"You do not know what I was going to say."

"Yes, I do. I learned it from you. And the answer to your next question is we work on it. To keep it fresh. Both of us. I don't have a mistress."

"I know that," he said with scorn. After a few more minutes and a refill, he said, "My marriage was arranged by our families. If you...."

"I won't write it down."

He sighed. "My wife gave me two children and it was over. We were civil. Sometimes fond. Like Sally, she was beautiful to look at, but also like Sally, she refused reality. It frightened her too much."

I thought about the brave young woman I suspected was now under consideration for the post. Alex was my old boss's daughter and not so beautiful, also not much older than Theresa was now, back when I met her in Chicago a dozen years ago. She would have to be very brave indeed, I thought, to marry this man. I took another sip of my coffee.

"You didn't dislike your wife as much as you do Sally, though, did you?" I asked.

"No. She disbelieved, but she grew up understanding the need for security. She was not a danger. She was just not... there. Sally is worse than a danger. You were present when she said she does not care if he dies. She is malignant. And she has access."

I nodded. "I was the one who explained that concept to Alex."

"Her father explained access to her, because of Vasily's father."

"Yes. He explained what it was. I told her what it meant. I told her she would have to go with Vasily."

I poured us another cup. I knew what he wanted, and I gave it with the coffee. "Alex understands access. She knows reality, loyalty, and responsibility. The religion thing strengthens her; it doesn't weaken her like it does some. She is not squeamish about life."

"She was squeamish in Chicago."

I was in the dark here. I badly wanted to know what he meant, but I could not ask. Instead, I said the first thing I could think of. "She was very young, Mack."

"She was," he agreed.

"Louis told a witness in Chicago last year," I said, "that you cried over your wife's coffin."

It was an incongruity given our current conversation and I am too much an intelligence officer to let such things go. I feared I could almost hear that dangerous stillness settling in him, but to my surprise, he answered.

"No," he said. "Not Katya. Nadia, my daughter. Louis also was not himself that day and so misremembered. Nadia was everything a father could wish, dutiful, kind, obedient, beautiful, a talented dancer, and not too intelligent. I always thought a touch of stupidity in a woman helps to make her compliant. Until I met Sally."

"Too much of either can have the opposite effect," I said.

"But your women are very intelligent, and they comply well enough."

I wondered which women he meant. "With you, yes," I said. "They have a fair amount of common sense. Sometimes they even listen to me."

I thought he was having difficulty processing this latest admission of my inadequacy as a man controlling his women because he paused the conversation for so long.

"I am sorry there will be no marriage between Theresa and my son," he said finally with some reluctance.

There were so many ways to unpack these words, my mind could not decide on a favorite, so I thought instead about how happy I was by their practical import. Theresa would not wed a young, reckless killer and womanizer like I knew his father had been at his age, and then be locked up in some mountain fastness on the other side of the world with three other killers, one way more reckless and two-way more experienced, and all three of them too interested in women and not in a platonic way. I found I was delighted with this news and did my best to hide it.

"It's not a problem," I said.

"But if she is pregnant…."

"She won't be. Maryann had the doctor put her on the pill more than a year ago."

"But she was a virgin. Louis...."

Of course, Louis would know this. I wished I was physically capable of killing him. Mentally, I was quite capable.

"We were not about to let biology derail her career," I said. "She is heading for medical school."

I think he was honestly shocked.

"It is a different world," he said finally.

"It is," I agreed. "I rather like it."

TWENTY-SIX

We were home shortly before four on Tuesday morning, and I hoped it was the last morning. Maryann had fresh coffee ready and greeted me at the kitchen door wearing her oldest bathrobe and a patient expression. Her luxuriant chestnut hair with its merest touch of grey stood out at all angles. I greeted her with total gratitude, and not just for the coffee.

"Almost over," I murmured in her ear as I hugged her. She smiled.

Jay sat at the kitchen table, eating.

Mack pushed his way in, looked around the room, and said, "Where is Sally?"

Jay swallowed his food and told him he had put a watcher on her door.

"In the house? A watcher in the house?" Mack nearly shouted it. For him, I mean. It registered just above normal conversational volume.

"He is not armed and he will stay inside until it's over," said Jay through a mouthful of biscuit.

Mack allowed himself to be mollified with bad grace, ignored the proffered mug from Maryann, and pushed me through the living room door ahead of him. I heard Louis and Steve enter the kitchen behind us.

My daughter, the future doctor, was sitting in a chair before the sensor radio console, wearing a headset and listening for signals denoting intruders. Charlie came in from the hallway. He had a silent communication with his father that manifested itself in the merest chin lift and meant Sally was where she should be because Mack visibly relaxed.

O-four-something is the perfect time for a meeting, especially if nobody has slept, everybody is armed, and most are facing at least the possibility of death in the next few hours. Mack took my seat at the head of the table for the first time. I took his seat on the right. Things had changed.

Maryann provided coffee, biscuits, and bacon, piled on trays. Nobody used plates. The time for niceties had passed. Crumbs were swept to the floor to make room for the plan of Steve's house and neighborhood to be unrolled across the dining room table. Theresa and the sensor console were brought into the room so that all she had to do was raise her hand to get instant attention. Maryann was asked to stay, to her surprise and evident mistrust. She sat opposite Mack, near the kitchen door.

"Beauregard, or Richard Bertram, has a seventeen-year-old son named David," said Louis, beginning a discussion of the personnel records.

Heads swiveled to Theresa. She was busy filing her nails and could not hear what was said because of the headset. The Brat walked over to where she sat near the living room door and snapped his fingers. She looked up. I knew better than to launch myself at the arrogant son of a bitch. He was so like his father. She took off the headset.

"That nerdy friend of yours, with the computer games, what is his name?" said Charlie. The emphasis he placed on the word friend told me something. Was he jealous? Also, where did he learn the word nerdy? From Steve?

"David. I told you. David Bertram. He's very smart. He graduated with my class, but he is a year younger."

Lucky for him he is still a minor, I thought, or he'd get no older.

No one else in The Section had a seventeen-year-old son named David. The other two Lindas had no sons at all. Compelling, but not conclusive, as far as evidence goes, I thought. Then Louis moved on from personnel to the computer, describing in detail how he had accessed each compartmented file.

Luckily, those files were only summaries. I had moved all details and sources away from the central system in The

Section when I got back from Chicago. I wanted to make it as difficult as possible to access certain critical information.

"Unfortunately," said Louis, "those files were only summaries with no details or sources, but I was able to locate the file for last year's CETUS WEDGE operation on a separate server, and I was not the first to do so." He looked me in the eye as he said this, telling me how useless that little security measure had been. It inconvenienced no one except those who legitimately needed the information.

"The file is located on a server in another part of the building," Louis said, "but both the server and the terminal in the vault communicate through a mainframe computer in another building on the campus. All communications are secure. There is no communication off the campus unless it is manually uploaded from a physical storage medium.

"The Cetus Wedge file contained the ballistic signature that was determined to belong to Steve's Smith & Wesson at the end of that op. That information was changed two days ago. The change was accomplished on the terminal in the vault, according to the history files of the terminal."

Louis paused, like a judge about to pronounce sentence, which in a way he was. I noticed that Theresa was all attention, with her hand holding one earpiece of the headset to her ear, leaving the other ear free to listen.

"There is a logbook just inside the door of the vault," continued Louis. "An electronic record is made any time the vault is opened. If there is no signature on the log matching

the time of the electronic record, it will trigger an investigation. Steve explained this to me and signed your name to the
log."

"Thanks, Steve." I meant it. I had forgotten this bit of
minutiae.

"Two nights ago, at almost the same hour, Richard
Bertram signed the log," said Louis.

"I can't believe he would know how to turn a computer
on," I said, "let alone change a file."

"He did not," said Louis. "I gained access to the video
files of the hallways that are kept in the system. They are on
a sixty-hour loop. The video of Bertram opening the vault
door has not been erased." He held up a video cassette. "His
son is clearly with him as he enters the vault. You will need
this."

Louis handed me the cassette. Evidence does not get
much more definitive than that. I set it on the table before me
and stared at it.

"It should be both," said Jay, ever the cop. I looked up
sharply. He raised heavy eyebrows at me.

Maryann's eyes widened and I realized she knew we
were talking about death.

"He's seventeen," I said.

"Old enough in some states," said Jay.

Mack was looking at me. "He will come for you later," he
said. "He will come for them." He pointed to Maryann and
Theresa.

"To hell with later," said Jay. "He's an accomplice to murder right now."

Must be nice to be blind to ambiguity.

"What? No!" said Theresa. "He's my friend." So she knew, too. I was rather proud of my intelligent women.

"Do you have enough to gain the commission?" Mack asked me.

"Yes." I sighed, then admitted, "For both."

"Will you ask for both?"

"Dad, no!"

"You say he is just a friend?" said Charlie.

Theresa froze. She heard the menace, the tinge of jealousy, and instinct told her Charlie would not worry about Jay's desire for justice or Mack's insistence on the sanction of a properly constituted commission, or my propensity for moral deliberation.

"You wanted a dangerous man," I mumbled.

"It appears she has two," said Louis, chuckling.

Mack spoke to me again. "You must tell them now, and you must decide."

"There is no question about the older Bertram. I will ask for that commission. There is sufficient evidence for the son as well...."

"Dad, are you judge and jury? How can you? It's not even a fair fight. And he's seventeen and a friend of mine."

"Do you want me to give him a fair fight, Theresa?" said Charlie. "Do you think he will win?"

His tone was soft, but his words held all the venom he intended and Theresa aged a decade with that new understanding.

"Tell them," said Mack.

I took a deep breath, moved down the table to a chair next to Theresa, and looked at a blank spot on the wall before me. I began a full and truthful confession, publicly, to everyone in the room. All but two already knew the story, because they had been there. For my wife and daughter, it wasn't just a confession of my part in the deaths of Charlie's sister and mother, Mack's wife and daughter. It was a revelation to them of my real occupation, of what I had been doing all my adult life to put a roof over our heads, of the dirty universe I had fought to keep as far away from that roof and my world as I could and which was presently sitting at my dining room table discussing a thing called a commission.

Maryann closed her eyes, opened them, and said, "And now you are asked to make a judgment that may affect the lives of your wife and daughter." She sighed and hung her head for a moment. "For myself, Leo," she said looking up at me with the directness I knew and loved so well, "I would rather face a danger in the future than kill a boy in the present. But I want to protect my daughter as well. I am tempted to say at any cost."

"Dad," said Theresa quietly, "I would help you if you committed a murder, even if it made me an accomplice."

I sighed and hung my head "Then be an accomplice in a non-murder, and, I hope, to multiple non-murders." I took her hand and turned her to face me. "I'm sure you know better than to blab about the people you've met this weekend, but I want more than that. I want perfect silence about how you spent the holiday, down to every little detail. No references to 'someone said,' no descriptions of anything anywhere anytime. Describe a fantasy novel as far removed from this as possible, but nothing else. That includes not one mention or even an oblique reference, no knowing smiles, no blushes, and I know this will cost you considerable cachet among your friends, but there must be absolutely nothing about Charlie."

I felt the room stiffen, and it was my turn to look at each of the team and smile, especially at the Frenchman.

"You guys didn't know that was one of my duties, did you?" I said. "I'm the guy who neutralizes the pillow talk and cleans up the information sieve you invariably leave behind."

Louis shrugged. "Who has time to talk? Misha especially has no conversation."

Misha threw him a sharp glance.

"The SIG in his holster speaks volumes," I said and turned back to Theresa. As my eyes swept across the table, I did not miss the sly looks exchanged between Charlie and Steve. *Donovan is not going to miss Sally very much, after all.*

I continued. "All of this is vital, sweetie, but it goes a thousand percent for David. You must never, ever speak of this to him, and you must stop speaking to him at all, casually and gradually, but very soon. None of us will attend the funeral because we will be out of town on a previously arranged trip to somewhere. You will start college as planned but transfer elsewhere next semester. We'll discuss that later. Can you abide by everything I've said?"

"You know I can, Dad, I'm not stupid."

Maryann also nodded, with a slight smile for her daughter, whom she then pulled from the room to help her with Danny, upstairs crying for his breakfast.

I picked up the disk on the table and looked at Mack. "I will call my boss," I said. "It will be only Beauregard."

He acknowledged this with a single nod. "And Potemkin Village," he said.

"Of course."

It was just after five o'clock.

TWENTY-SEVEN

I t took about two minutes to secure the commissions. That was a minute and a half for one rogue babysitter and thirty seconds for Potemkin Village. Uncle Sam is not fond of hostile specialist teams who show up on American soil uninvited.

I nodded at Mack as I entered the dining room. He was leaning over the plan Steve had drawn of his home and the cul-de-sac that surrounded it.

"For fuck's sake," said Charlie. "Where did you learn to draw, Steve? Your son would have done a better job with a sharp crayon."

Charlie was learning some new American idioms from Steve. These were markedly different from those he heard from Alex. I had to admit the criticism was apt though. Drunken rectangles lined a crooked street that ended in even more inebriated squares connected in a row of four. An X marked the second square from the right. Rough circles tried and failed to depict rows of hedges and bushes between each of the townhouses and surrounding the front and back of Steve's unit.

"How tall?" said Mack, pointing to the row of circles to the right of the house.

"About seven feet."

A pause, a stare, and Steve looked at the ceiling while he calculated. "A little over two meters," he said.

"And here?" Mack pointed at the squiggles to the left.

"Uh, I can see the top of the guy next door's head, and he's shorter than I am."

Neatly done, I thought. Steve left the conversion to Mack. I wanted Mack to ask him how much shorter the man was just for the pleasure of watching Steve convert inches to centimeters.

"These?" Mack was asking about a row of circles clustered along the front of the house.

"They reach to about halfway up the front window."

"What were you thinking, Steve?" I couldn't help it. He had been in the game for only about a year and had some really good instincts, but this house was boneheaded.

"I like the privacy," he said. "You can't see in from the street."

"And you can't see out to find who's hiding in the bushes," I said. "Curtains will give you privacy, for God's sake." I suspected Sally had something to do with it, but she was already not a favorite person in Mack's eyes, so I let it drop. So did Steve, with a grateful look. I had saved him from another calculation.

Another large paper was unrolled and the china cabinet raided for four fine crystal goblets to weigh down the corners. This chart illustrated Steve's inability to draw the inside of a house. He had the sofa roughly drawn in at one end of a room that served as both living and dining room.

"Where do you eat?" asked Mack.

Steve waved vaguely toward the other end of the ground floor room.

"At a table?" said Mack, as still and as quiet as I had ever seen him. I wanted to slip out but dared not move. Neither did anybody else.

"Um. Yeah. I...."

Mack's fist hit the table hard enough to topple two glasses over onto the polished surface, chipping one, and a third completely off the table and onto the floor, where it shattered. There followed a blistering stream of German invective listing all of Steve's inadequacies, from the choice of Sally—a point that still rankled, it seemed—to the house covered in bushes, his inability to understand so simple a system of measurement a five-year-old can do it, his impudence, his sloppy care of his new weapon, the state he keeps his holster in, his despicable table manners—I wondered about the materiality of this one in the lifestyle of a specialist—and his utter inattention to details.

I realized Steve was standing like a statue, glanced to my right, and saw Jay in the same stance. They were both Air Force Academy graduates, presumably accustomed to this sort of thing. Jay didn't speak the language, but he knew a dressing down when he heard one.

Mack sat down again and spoke in English, reasonably calm given the topic. "We must know every detail of a space we enter, as accurately as possible, or we die. Things go wrong. The more we do not know, the more things go wrong. Get that into your brain. Let it become part of your spine. Ignorance kills!"

Steve pulled the paper toward him and took out a pen. "I'll…"

"No," said Mack. "There is no time and they will blow it up anyway."

Steve stared at him open-mouthed, a silent "How…?" dying on his lips.

"Why have a man like Todor if you do not use him? He is a slow fighter and a mediocre shot." Mack looked at me. "If we had Sobieski, we could save the houses. He would also tell us how they might detonate. And he could fight."

I gratefully counted this as mild criticism compared to what had been dished out to Steve. I had been partly responsible for Sobieski's death as well as those of Mack's wife and daughter.

To Jay, Mack said, "Did you move the people out of the houses nearby?"

"I moved everybody out of the cul-de-sac. There are three single-story houses backing up to the rear fence along the townhouses. I moved those people also."

I wondered if I could steal Jay from the FBI. It was not fair they had somebody like him and I didn't. He was compromised, yes, but oh so competent.

"Watchers?" asked Mack.

"I have mine in the house directly behind. I can neutralize Potemkin's watchers out on the street. We know who they are."

"Do so. They know we know." He stood over the first diagram and looked over his shoulder at Louis seated behind and to his right. Louis stood, looked down at it, and murmured something to Mack, who indicated the blank area on the left side of the cul-de-sac and asked Steve, "What is the terrain like? What is here?"

"The ground slopes up from the street," said Steve, no doubt in approved military fashion. "It's quite steep, about forty degrees, covered in waste brush, scrub trees, loose baseball-sized rocks, grass, and weeds. There is a street at the top, about thirty feet higher than the street in the cul-de-sac. Distance from street to street I would say is sixty-five feet."

That was a first-rate answer, detailed, precise, and knowledgeable. He had to do it over in meters. And then define baseball-sized.

Mack and Louis spoke quietly.

"Michael," said Mack, "where will Dani Suta set up his rifle?"

Charlie thought for only a moment. "On the high ground directly across from the house, so he will slant northeast, with morning sun at the earliest time at the front. He can hit a fly on a wall at two thousand meters, so he will not understand the need for cover from so close a range."

Louis chuckled. "He will lug all that long-distance equipment for no reason. Misha will take care of him in a few seconds."

"Back up?" asked Mack.

Charlie considered. "I'd say one on either side, some seven meters down the slope. And there will be a radio. He is famous for answering with a grunt."

This level of precision intelligence astounded me. In that instant, I learned a dozen truths, the foremost being the sheer volume and detail of information these guys needed just to stay alive. Next was their consummate skill in gathering the intelligence. Finally, I knew in my gut that in accessing a server by going through our main frame, the Frenchman had vacuumed the main frame. Gathering everything available would have been impossible, but he took anything we produced about operations conducted by other teams or terrorist organizations, first the hostiles, then friendlies they had their doubts about.

It must have registered across my face. I realized no one was speaking and all were looking at me.

"Do you have a complaint?" asked Mack.

"When one has been well and truly fucked," I said, "there is no use in complaining about the last stroke."

"If it is the last," murmured Jay next to me.

"Now you know what we require," said Mack. "That is why we invited you and Jay to this meeting, so you will understand what we require for the future, if we live, and for the present, which we will address now."

I had wondered why Jay and I were there. I never before had been privy to their planning, but usually was just ordered to perform this, that, and the other thing now, in the next ten minutes, and an hour ago, depending on urgency.

"What are the numbers, Jay?" asked Mack.

"Four fighters, including Suta, from Potemkin Village, plus Todor Chilikov and four rentals who are at best mediocre, but can fire an AK-47."

"Is this information good?"

"The best. The man who rented them out to them is an acquaintance."

"How?"

"We grew up in the same neighborhood. He is now a gang leader here. He does not lie to me."

"Can he call them back?"

Jay shook his ponderous head. "He wants them gone. That's why he rented them out. You are doing him a favor."

"Are they black?" Mack's brow was furrowed. It would be an easy way to identify them in this neighborhood.

"No."

"You will need another babysitter, perhaps Skosh, for cleanup," Mack said to me.

I opened my mouth to protest.

"Unless I am dead, you will have other things to do."

Arguments die under the weight of some statements. "I'll call and put him on standby," I said.

There were more increasingly detailed and rehearsed instructions. Steve was made to repeat his instructions three times.

"Your strength is in unarmed combat," Mack told him. "I do not want you to be near enough to use it. Shoot. Fast. Relentless."

Steve nodded.

"If they plan to blow up the house, and you are the targets," said Jay, "how do they plan to get you in there?"

After a general, uncomfortable silence, Steve said, "My wife."

"How can they use her?"

"Through fear and deception," said Mack. "Have you made arrangements to take the child?"

Jay nodded. "Just as soon as they're awake."

"No," said Mack. "Now. Take the child now."

But it was already too late.

It was just before six o'clock.

TWENTY-EIGHT

Theresa found her mother when she handed the headset to the watcher and went to the kitchen for coffee. Maryann lay sprawled under the table, her head toward the refrigerator, a significant bleeding gash at her temple. A can of green beans lay beside her. Theresa raised the alarm.

In forty-five seconds, the dining room was in chaos and unrecognizable. If a gun existed that could scratch my table, it was doing so, with help from high-capacity magazines, suppressors, belts, knives, radios, and other paraphernalia.

Maryann regained consciousness, pointed to the key rack, and started another pot of coffee. The keys to my car were gone, along with both Sally and the baby. The mess of Danny's breakfast had not yet congealed on the high chair tray. Louis disinfected and bandaged Maryann's temple. He offered her a questionable European pain reliever, but she took a couple of ibuprofen from a small kitchen drawer instead, then ran upstairs and threw on a t-shirt, jeans, and a pair of sneakers.

The team got dressed without undue modesty, despite Theresa and Maryann, now bandaged, streaming in and out of the kitchen door with more biscuit, egg, and bacon sandwiches, heated in the microwave, so almost fresh, and pots of coffee.

Maryann stopped to stare once until I cleared my throat. She put the hot coffee pot on the unprotected table, something she normally never would do, and scurried back to the kitchen. I put a placemat under the pot. Theresa's eyes were wider than I had ever seen them and no amount of throat-clearing made her avert them. She stood with a platter of biscuits until Maryann called her from the kitchen, then placed it on the table between two MP5 submachine guns and backed to the door before leaving and returning with more food.

The Brat took a beautiful Ferlach custom-made sniper rifle from its case, checked the mounts on the scope, inserted a magazine, screwed on a suppressor, chambered a round, and sited the scope before he noticed Theresa watching him. She held the now empty coffee pot in her hand. He gave her a somewhat rueful smile, donned his magazine-laden belt and Glock, then shrugged on a black jacket.

I was given grunting lessons by Louis, who had heard an actual sample of Suta's radio discourse. How I was to come into possession of his radio was not explained to me until they were just about to leave.

"If they have the woman," said Mack, evidently unable to force her name through his lips, "they know now about you, Maryann, and Theresa. You will take them with you in the pink minivan." He gave me instructions for a rendezvous point on the block beyond the ridge road, behind a convenience store. Jay and his watcher were to meet us there. My house would remain undefended.

The scratches on my dining table became trivial.

The team all wore close-fitting black clothing, with enough stretch to allow full range of movement, sturdy boots, and looser-fitting jackets. The automatic rifles and submachine guns were slung over their shoulders or across their backs. Charlie carried his rifle.

They filed through the kitchen, past the sink full of dishes, around the open dishwasher, through the garage door, and into the Mercedes parked inside, pausing only to put spare gear into the trunk next to the first aid kit and another radio set.

My family and I followed them, in t-shirts, jeans, light jackets, earplugs, and worried looks. I wore a shoulder rig with my Walther PPK under my jacket. We climbed into the minivan, and I clicked the garage door opener. Jay and his watcher were already on the road waiting.

We all took different routes to the convenience store and rolled in at about six-twenty. The front passenger, back, and

side doors of the van opened. Jay replaced Maryann as my
passenger. She moved next to Theresa in the back, with
Mack on the floor across their feet. The other three arranged
themselves in the very back, staying low, with comments
about the crap allowed to live there, like a beach umbrella
and a tennis bag, both of which were passed to Maryann and
arranged somewhere on the back seat. Maryann lost her reserve and became herself again, so she gave as good as she
got, telling them what she thought of beggars trying to be
choosy. The watcher, a junior special agent, stayed in Jay's
car to manage radio traffic, a couple of jamming bursts, and
the FBI car phone. He was also responsible for the security of
the Mercedes.

Mack directed every turn from the floor behind me and
had me park slanted-in toward the curb on the side of the
road above the cul-de-sac, nose pointed at the townhouses
below. Despite an abundance of scrub trees and low brush,
the view was excellent. My car was parked below in front of
Steve's house behind his silver minivan. When the hell had
Mack checked out the neighborhood sufficiently to be this
precise, I wondered, and how did he do so without the thousand and one watchers in the area noticing?

"What about their babysitter?" I said, staring straight
ahead. "Have we accounted for him?"

"He will not be here. Babysitters do not participate," said
Mack.

"What the fuck am I doing here then?"

"You are learning the bad speech habits of Steve. It is good I am taking him from you. Now listen."

There followed detailed and minute instructions to govern me for the next sixty seconds, followed by the least welcome of all strictures.

"If we fail," he said, "you must take Maryann and Theresa to your safe place and contact Alex. She will get you out of the country."

He knew about the safe place. He knew I could contact Alex. "My government...."

"You are your government, Frank. If we fail, you will have failed. No one can repair that. Get out."

I thought he meant out of the country. Before I could put up another argument, he hissed, "Now!"

I complied. As casually as possible, I climbed out of the driver's seat and meandered down the side of the van, watching the ground near the edge of the road, searching for something that must have fallen out some thirty feet back— otherwise expressed as ten meters. I made a great show of spotting something and picking it up. Satisfied, I turned and headed back, still watching the ground, spotted another something at the edge of the brush after about two and a half meters, bent to pick *it* up, and saw Mack take out Suta, the sniper.

It was fast, absolutely silent, and horrifying.

The next thing I knew, he was stuffing a pistol into my belt, a firing pin in one hand, and a radio up the sleeve of my other arm. It's not like I hadn't seen the results of his work a bunch of times. I was just never present to see the process, that's all, and I never want to be again. My paralysis lasted less than a millisecond though, so I was able to stop the radio falling out of my sleeve, shift the pistol to a more secure position, and saunter seamlessly back to the car.

Once in my seat, I reached behind Jay to give my wife the things we wanted any watchers to believe she had dropped and I had retrieved.

"What is this?" she asked, holding out the firing pin.

"Just keep it, I'll explain later." I had turned forward again by this time and in my side mirror saw a long rifle barrel resting on the seat back behind Theresa and past her ear, its suppressor extending a few inches through the open window.

"I thought you were going to take Suta's position," I said quietly.

Charlie snorted softly. "He was accustomed to being further back. He knew nothing about effective cover. The place is completely exposed."

I would not have said completely exposed, having walked past it in total ignorance, a state in which I would have happily remained had I not followed the instruction to pick up a stone just where I did. I suppose cover is in the eye of the beholder.

"Daddy."

"Yes, baby."

"I'm scared."

"I know sweetheart, but Charlie is very, very good at this and will be careful. You will hear it, but it has a suppressor so it won't shatter your ears."

"I have two in the hedge on the right and a third on the left down below. I think Papa will take down the one on the left when he gets there."

"What about the other two on the slope?" asked Jay.

"He will have taken them out by now," said Charlie.

"Todor?" I asked.

"I do not see him. With him, that makes three not visible. He will not be in the house. That means there are only two in the house with Sally. They are rentals. Easy for Louis and Steve. Todor will be in a place where he can detonate by radio."

It occurred to me that Louis and Steve must have exited the van while I was walking behind it. I never heard a thing.

There was a squawk on the radio I held, asking for Dani. I grunted into it. The radio seemed mollified and quieted, but not for long. Jay watched a stopwatch for three more seconds, then shouted into his radio, "Now!" and the most unholy blanket jamming of all transmissions in the area made us both squelch our radios at the same time. It lasted thirty seconds, during which time gunfire erupted below us.

We could not pinpoint the suppressed MP5s in the din, but the AKs boomed in long bursts from inside the house and from our left. Sally ran out the front door, dragging little

Danny by the hand. One of the tangos in the hedge on the right emerged and grabbed her arm, putting the muzzle of a handgun to her head. She let go of Danny's hand and he ran toward the silver minivan on the street as fast as his stubby little legs could carry him. He was chasing the neighbor's cat, which ran under the car. I heard the whizz-boom noise of the large suppressor behind my right ear and the skull of the man holding Sally exploded, forthwith.

Theresa said, "I'm going to be sick."

"Not yet. Hold still," said Charlie.

The house blew up and Danny was still on his way to the minivan as it also blew up before him in sympathy. A gun battle developed on the right between Steve and the hedge. As the child moved closer to the now burning car, Louis streaked from behind Steve on those long legs of his, tackled the boy, and covered him with his body.

The shooter in the hedge moved just outside his cover for a fraction of a second, which was enough time for Charlie. The man went down, not before hitting Louis at least once. Theresa threw up. Maryann held steady, though a little green, but she did not have the straight line of sight Theresa had.

There was no more gunfire. There was the crackling of the houses that were now all alight, and the cars, both the minivan and my car behind it. There was the eerie silence that always accompanies death. And of course, there were smells: of smoke and gasoline and cordite and blood.

I saw nothing more because I was speeding down the road and into the cul-de-sac. Jay was busy on the radio, asking for the standby surgeon to meet us at my house, asking Harkon to set up a perimeter, calling off the many sirens we could already hear from emergency vehicles, explaining they were not needed. He handed me his radio and I was patched through to Skosh. He would be here in four minutes to meet Harkon. I would be gone in less than three. An FBI watcher pulled up alongside us and took Maryann, Theresa, Sally, and the baby up to the back of the convenience store where they transferred into Jay's car.

We folded the back seats down and the team arranged itself along Louis's prone body, taking turns keeping pressure on a bullet wound that was too far up his leg at the back and inside and bled too much for my comfort. Louis lay on his stomach cracking bad jokes.

We stopped at the cars where Steve and Charlie took possession of the Mercedes and led us to my house.

There was no shortage of hands to carry Louis into the dining room, and I suddenly didn't give a shit that the magazines in his belt were scratching the hell out of my once fine table.

TWENTY-NINE

S ally tried to have a snit the moment she got in the door. Steve shut that right down. He tried to make her help the surgeon alongside Theresa, but she had a fit of the vapors. All that blood and stuff. Then we suggested she help Maryann fetch and carry whatever the doctor needed but had not brought with him. She did so with enough bad grace that Maryann gave up asking. Little Danny needed attention. His hair was singed and there was a blister on his forehead. The doctor gave Sally a salve for the blister and she took the boy into the kitchen, tended him, and fed him. She was competent to do that much.

Maryann washed Louis down after we stripped him and determined how we would hold him. Anesthetic was not on the cards. It was against the team's policy to be unconscious during an operation—their kind of operation, that is, not the medical kind. As far as they were concerned until they were out of US airspace, they were still operational.

Theresa set up a tea trolley with clean towels and the doctor's instruments, still sterile in their wrappers and laid out neatly, and assisted him throughout the ordeal. The rest of us held Louis still. He is a powerful guy. It wasn't easy.

I had seen them shot up, burned, hobbling on broken bones, vomiting blood, and peering through beaten faces. I had never seen them endure the treatment necessary to put them back together, not for something this serious. That usually took place on their well-equipped airplane where I was not invited.

Louis said nothing. He had been given the proverbial strip of leather to bite down on, cut from one of my best belts, which Maryann brought downstairs for the purpose. There were a few grunts and the veins stood out on the straining muscles of his arms, shoulders, neck, and legs.

The femoral artery was unaffected, but just barely. The damage was deep and though no bones were broken, the torn muscle would be painful for a long time. It took the doctor an hour to staunch the bleeding, remove the bullet, disinfect the wound, and suture the layers of tissue and skin. The team allowed an antibiotic but took it from their own medical kit in the trunk of the Mercedes.

Louis had begun to drift in and out of sleep by the time the last stitch was knotted. Maryann folded a clean bath towel, put it under his head, and covered him with a blanket. Mack sat in a chair, legs splayed out before him, filthy, disheveled, and exhausted. I sat next to him, in better physical shape, but mentally destroyed.

Charlie and Steve came in having washed and changed into clean shirts and sport coats. "We'll take care of it, Papa," said Charlie. "Steve must do it."

"Yes," said Steve.

Mack agreed with the merest nod.

I gathered my wits and said, "I'm going with them. I have to debrief him first." He raised an eyebrow. "Charlie and Steve will be there," I said. "They'll brief you," He gave a half smile.

On our way out to the garage, we met Jay in the kitchen, in the refrigerator actually, pulling out a platter of leftover biscuit sandwiches from breakfast. Sally glared at her husband from a chair in a corner, holding his sleeping son in her arms.

"We picked up Todor on his way to the airport," said Jay. "We had to put him on the airplane home. Turns out there is no law against carrying a radio."

"Ah, that is where your people and my people diverge my friend. Can I convince you to come over to the dark side? We offer good pay and benefits."

"Like hell you do. I'll stay on this side of the law, more or less."

"Sometimes it seems more less than more by your own choice."

"Choices can be tricky, but at least on this side, I can sometimes sleep at night."

I rode in the back of the Mercedes after Steve took my PPK and patted me down. We argued about how we were going to manage this. Steve wanted to just go in and blast away. Charlie was sympathetic but more receptive to my reasoned approach.

"Don't be such a fucking cowboy, Steve," I said. "This is not the OK Corral and I'm not Wyatt Earp. You'll end up getting me and my family killed if you don't listen to me, and I take exception to that. I'm glad you're alive and I hope you'll be comfortable in the blackest of black worlds, but I have no desire to join you. As somebody who should know told me recently, I have neither the skills nor the resources to survive there. Go with God, my boy, but leave me behind in some semblance of safety. Love, Frank." I kissed the air.

Charlie turned to look at me with a furrowed brow and a skeptical expression. "What do you suggest?" he said.

"One of you should go up to the front door and ask him to come with you. Bring him here. It's important that David, especially, does not see me. He must not associate this with Theresa." I knew that point would register with Charlie.

"What if he's armed?" he said. "It's not like we can pat him down in the street without inviting comment."

"True. Give me back my Walther and I'll cover him."

"I'll turn around and cover him," said Steve.

It was like I never knew him; he was so completely one of them.

Charlie went up to the house, no doubt with his most winning smile, and poured on the charm to Linda, but would not come in, with the best manners imaginable I was sure. When Beauregard surfaced, Charlie asked him to step outside, which he did with curiosity all over his face, having never seen this guy, who was too young to be one of Charlemagne. They were halfway to the car when he noticed it, blanched, faltered, and tried to turn. Charlie was ready for this and kept a firm grip on his arm, his Glock poking a hole in Beau's ribs. He opened the back door and shoved him in.

Beauregard found himself seated next to me, which surprised him, but not as much as the Beretta staring him in the face with Steve behind it with his finger in the trigger guard.

"I never meant...."

Charlie pulled the car away from the curb.

"It doesn't matter what you meant, Beau," I said. "I want to know what you did. Tell me about the Chinese."

He had dropped a bug in somebody's ear at one of his wife's great-uncle's dinners and was shocked, absolutely shocked, when he was contacted by somebody, some Chinese guy, with a briefcase full of money. He never meant....

"Cut the crap," I said. "What did you do then?"

The guy who gave him the briefcase also gave him the name and number of a guy. Really, he didn't expect the guy to try to blow up Steve's car. "I mean, my God, the baby!"

"Yeah, yeah," I said. "Why? What were you after?"

"I wanted Steve out of The Section," he said, trying very hard not to look at the Beretta. "He has no business there. He's not suited and he has no desire to learn from more experienced men. I thought I'd just scare him off. I've never been fully utilized in my opinion...."

His use of the word utilize was almost reason enough for the commission in my book, but I am an extremist.

"Linda agrees I'm under-appreciated," he continued nervously. "I worked so hard all my life and I'm never going any further. I'll retire soon and then what? I just wanted to scare him. Honest, that's all."

"Who suggested the Chinese?" This was a shot in the dark. I have no idea why I asked it.

"Linda said I should ask her uncle."

Steve and Charlie did not even raise an eyebrow at this prime intelligence. I made a mental note to call the guy on the China desk from a secure phone. I also sincerely hoped Charlie took Linda's involvement as just that of a silly woman trying to help her husband.

"And when it went wrong?" I said.

Beauregard's hands were shaking. He had been approached by somebody who knew all about it. Said to call him Nick. He could see Beau was in a bad situation, said Nick, and he had the surefire solution. He'd take care of the China problem and the Steve problem in one simple operation, and he asked nothing in return, absolutely nothing. Beauregard didn't think he had any choice, especially after Barcode. Nick knew about Barcode, too.

"Why Barcode?" I asked. "Why'd you kill him?"

"David thought it would be good to give you a different suspect, so we came up with a plan, and he's a genius with the computers, did you know that, Buddy? I'm so proud of him."

Theresa had said she'd help me if I committed a murder, but I don't think she would ever suggest it. I had a sour taste in my mouth about a lot of things right now.

I extracted a complete description of Nick and told Charlie to drop me off at a gas station. Steve gave me back my Walther. I took a taxi home. The Mercedes was already back in the garage and the last bags were being stuffed into the trunk, along with a diaper bag. The pink minivan was pressed into service once again, as Louis, dressed in a black warm-up suit he must have hated, was gently helped into the back, where he lay on his stomach for the ride. Mack sat next to him. I drove. Charlie and Steve took the Mercedes. Maryann, Theresa, Sally, and Danny rode with Jay.

I didn't know why my wife and daughter had been invited to the airfield, but I was glad they were staying in my sight. I could not bear to think of them alone in the house. I resolved then to find a place that is smaller, less conspicuous, and more easily secured.

At the airfield, it took some time to load all the gear and the injured man and to impart last-minute instructions and threats to me and Jay. I saw Charlie trying to take Theresa's hand. She pulled away. I recognized the hardening face of his father as he had been at that age and shuddered.

Sally sobbed all the way up the steps. Steve held Danny and talked airplanes with him as they went inside.

...

The house was quiet when we got home like it was sighing. The dining room table was a write-off and the crystal goblet still lay in pieces on the floor. Beds were all unmade, bathrooms filthy. The kitchen won the nightmare contest hands down, with dirty dishes everywhere, the dishwasher overflowing, and the refrigerator decimated of food, but no shortage of the baby food that had dried and stuck to an abandoned highchair. Maryann handed me a very dirty martini, made one for herself, and we sat on the sofa in the living room, the only relatively unscathed room in the house.

"Leo," said Maryann.

"Yes, my most beautiful girl," I said, slipping an arm around her shoulder. The martini combined with the sheer volume of relief gave me ideas.

"I don't understand Sally at all. I understand better the violent men you had here. We're all capable of some of that, more or less. But Sally is almost more dangerous, wouldn't you say? To not believe anything that's said to her and to put everybody's life in danger because why? For no reason."

"She was afraid, Maryann, but you're right. Mack said it best. Fear and deception have robbed her of common sense."

"Do you think Mack will kill her?"

"He wants to, but I don't think he will because of Danny. There is only so much trauma a child can handle, especially one that young. Mack won't take his mother from him, at least, not yet."

We sipped companionably.

"Leo," she said again. "I have a confession to make."

I held my breath, waiting for some mention of that damned Louis.

"All those years," she continued, "you would go off for days or weeks and come home exhausted and you wouldn't talk about anything. Sometimes you did no more than grunt for hours. And often you wouldn't eat, even when I made your favorite dinner. I thought it was an affair. I was so hurt. There were times I didn't ever want to talk to you again, but we had young children and you were a good provider. Most important, you came around in a few days after each time and then you were right as rain until the next trip."

She took a healthy sip of her martini. "I'm sorry I ever doubted you. I'm sorry I was not more supportive during those times."

I took a deep breath. "You supported me, Maryann. I was always knee-deep in blood and filth and treachery and terror. It just took me a few days to surface again as a human being. It never would have been possible without you. Even Charlemagne thinks you are the best thing since sliced bread. I think they're a little jealous."

I didn't mention the Frenchman. I figured if I'm her type, he can't be, so why bring it up? Besides, she was sucking on her olive in a way that drove Charlemagne completely out of my thoughts.

...

They found Beauregard in a ditch not too far from his home. He had been shot execution style by someone who accepted instruction from a more experienced man.

"Family says he went off in a Mercedes," said Chief Harkon, as we looked down at the body. "They say a young blond guy came to the door and they started talking and just got in a black car. That's the last they saw of him."

We stood and contemplated the mystery.

"I just can't seem to shake the memory of a Glock 17 I saw from a very unhealthy angle," he continued. "Was that yesterday?"

"Yes."

"Seems like it was a long time ago. Anyway, the guy be-hind the Glock was kind of young, I'd say. Kind of blond, too."

"Very blond," I said, correcting him.

"You want me to do anything special about this dead guy? He's another one of your employees, I think."

I nodded. "Can you just let me have the ballistics report when you get it?"

"Sure. Mind if I ask? Is this the last one? I mean, is it over and are they gone?"

"They?"

"The killers you were hosting at your house."

I took a moment to answer, deciding on a touch of truth. "Yeah. They're gone, and it should be over." There are no guarantees in the black, I wanted to say, but I kept my mouth shut. I suspected he knew it, anyway.

"I'm thinking this guy," he used his chin to indicate the body before us, "killed the other guy from your unit."

"That's about right."

"Some workplace dispute, maybe."

I gave a half nod, half shake.

"When you say it should be over, I'm guessing it's not over for everybody. Maybe it's not over for you."

I closed my eyes. "No."

"But it's over for him." He looked down at Beauregard.

"Yes," I said. "It's over for him."

...

I put the Beretta's ballistic report in the Charlemagne file and sent a copy via FedEx to the accommodation address I had been given in a teeny tiny country in the Alps. The following week, I picked up from my own accommodation address a packet with all the information the Soviets had on The Section, as promised by Louis, and began tightening up our filing procedures, because nothing is ever over for us bureaucrats.

EPILOGUE

A servant led Sally silently down the hallway, along its strange eastern carpet, and opened a door at one end. Without making eye contact, he indicated that she should enter, then closed the door behind her. She stood in a bare room, high ceilinged like all the rooms in this place, and windowless, again like all the others she had seen.

Misha sat behind a large mahogany desk at the far end of the room. His chair, the desk, and a plain, straight-backed kitchen chair in front of the desk were the only furniture in the room. There were no decorations anywhere. The bare floor made an echo of her footsteps as she acquiesced to his gesture to sit in the kitchen chair facing him.

He looked at her through bloodshot eyes. His face held three days' growth of a beard, blond like his hair, with hints of grey blending in almost imperceptibly. He wore all black and reeked of blood and vomit. There was dried mud on the belt that held his SIG Sauer semiautomatic. His sleeves were up, exposing powerful scarred forearms. He placed his palms flat on the polished surface of the desk.

She summoned defiance. He gave her contempt.

"What do you want?" she said. "Who do you think you are locking me up like this for the past week? I don't even know your real name."

"You may call me Satan. As you see, we have returned from England." He remained still and silent after this, until she began to fidget.

"I am told you have not asked to see your husband." His blue eyes seemed to pierce her skull.

"So?"

"You may be gratified to know he is expected to live."

She shrugged. "Great. Then we can go back to that hovel you put us in before. At least Danny can play outside there—when there isn't six feet of snow."

He continued to regard her silently.

"Why did we have to come back to this prison?" she demanded.

"While we were away, we needed to ensure your safety. This is the safest place. Were you not well cared for by the staff?"

"I don't believe you."

"That is your choice." He continued to stare at her.

It began to unnerve her. "What do you want?" she demanded again.

"I want to know what you want."

"You know what I want. I want to go home."

"Steve cannot go back. You know that."

"I know nothing of the kind. And his name is Dan. Get that through your thick skull."

Misha became very still and it unnerved her again. She did not know why he had that effect on her but elected to maintain her defiant return stare. Finally, he said, "Steve Donovan is his name. He is in my employ. Everything he has, everything you have, belongs to me and you will do me the courtesy of calling him Steve simply because I say you will!" The last word was accompanied by a fist pounded onto the top of the desk, making her jump involuntarily.

His voice became quieter, but she could not make herself relax. She fidgeted on the chair, trying and failing to find a more comfortable way to sit.

"I have a proposition for you," he said.

"I'm not giving up my son."

"He is Steve's son as well, but I will not ask you to give him up. Will you listen?"

She hesitated, suspecting a trap. "Ye-es."

"You cannot go home." He held up his hand as she opened her mouth to protest. "Unless you want your parents to participate in your danger."

"I'm not in any danger." She rolled her eyes.

"Very well, then. Go home to them, but the boy will not go. I will allow you to place your parents in peril, but not the child."

"It's no use talking to you, mister. You are a liar."

"A few months ago, a man held a gun to your head; your house and car were destroyed by explosives, and your son was nearly killed until my friend risked his life and indeed, took a serious bullet wound, saving the child. You were present for all of that. You saw it, you heard it, you smelled it. What part of it was a lie?"

She had no answer. She would have said it was all play-acting, as she knew it was, but the brains of the man with the gun had splattered against the side of her head and there was all that blood and…. She closed her eyes at the memory and tried to close her mind, comfortably, safely, but could not, which allowed his next words to enter.

"You may go anywhere you like, but not home. You will be able to call your parents as much as you wish. I will give you a telephone number to call that will keep them and you safe. Understand that I do not care about your safety. I care about the child. To that end, I will give you a house, a car, a modest income, and will cover all the expenses involved with raising the child, such as food, clothing, and school fees. You may pick any place east of the Mississippi River. There are stipulations. Are you prepared to hear them?"

"Yes."

He listed them, like items on a grocery list.

"You will do nothing to endanger the child. I do not mean that you will do nothing that you think will endanger him, but nothing that I think will do so. My opinion is the only one that counts. If you endanger him, Steve will take the child. You will never see him again, and all support will cease.

"If you elect to voluntarily allow the child to live with his father at a future date so that you may resume what you call a normal life, you will continue to receive the same support minus the child's expenses.

"You will resume your maiden name and call Danny by that name. I will provide the documents necessary to satisfy schools and other authorities.

"You will tell your parents, whom you may call as often as you wish, that you cannot say where you are because Dan, as you call him, works for the government in a secret job. You may give your parents the accommodation number I will provide so that you can receive calls, and when he is old enough, you may allow the child to speak to them, but you will never visit them nor give any hint of your location. If you do, Steve will take the boy and all support will cease.

"You will not disclose to anyone, at any time, Danny's true name or any of the details concerning the separation from your husband. You may say you are divorced and leave it at that. Is this clear to you?"

She nodded. "When can I leave?"

"Where do you wish to go?"

She thought. Geography had not been a strong subject for her. "Texas," she said.

"It is west of the Mississippi."

"Tennessee."

"No."

"You said!"

He raised an eyebrow.

"All right, all right. North Carolina?"

He considered it and nodded.

"When can I leave?" she asked again.

He opened a drawer on his right and drew out a small number of large papers, elaborately captioned and densely printed. He pushed one page toward her and offered a pen.

"What's this? I can't read this. What are you asking me to sign?"

"Your divorce," he said. "It will be granted by a court in Vienna before the end of the month. Sign where I have marked an X."

"I can't read it. It's written in some kind of gibberish; how do I know what it is? I don't trust you."

"You may trust me to kill you if you give me any more trouble."

It was the stillness in his manner, in his voice, in his staring blue eyes, that pierced the fog of her delusion just enough to make her act in her own best interest. She signed.

He took the paper and the pen, and said, "Go. Pack your things. You leave tonight."

The End

Will Charlie's plan keep Misha and Louis from destroying each other? Find out in *Lion Tamer*, the next installment of the Charlemagne Files, available here: https://books2read.com/u/4A2YAp

Join the Charlemagne Files newsletter for more stories and information about the series, its world of covert operations, and the lives of the characters on the team. Sign up at: https://www.charlemagnefiles.com/contact.

If you enjoyed this book, please consider leaving a short review at your favorite bookstore.

CHARLEMAGNE AND THE SECTION

The fictional world of The Section follows a few conventions. It may help the first-time reader of The Charlemagne Files to know some of these.

Who/what/ where is The Section?

The Section is a department of an intelligence agency of the United States. Its employees are civil servants. It includes support staff members who provide identity documents, financial controls, and physical and document security. The offices are near the East Coast, maybe Virginia.

The operational agents are called babysitters. They arrange on-site logistical support for freelance specialists during operations. Most operations are not conducted within the United States, with some exceptions.

Babysitters themselves do not carry identity documents in their names during an operation and never carry any official identification from their organization. Their purpose is to allow the organization to deny any association with them or their mission.

Nicknames

Babysitters in The Section receive nicknames from their coworkers when they join the office. These names are often undesirable and used mercilessly among the members of the office. It is part of the team-building process in a stressful occupation.

Coins

Challenge coins are traditionally stamped with symbols or mottos that designate the intelligence unit of their owners. The tradition is that when members of the unit are present at the bar and one produces his coin, all must produce theirs. Anyone failing to show their coin is responsible for the bar tab. If all produce their coins, then the challenger who first produced his or her coin is responsible for the tab.

File designations

The highest classification of information is Top Secret. Beyond Top Secret, more sensitive information is strictly controlled in a number of ways including designation as Sensitive Compartmented Information (SCI). This requires an additional clearance and often a named clearance based on Need-To-Know.

In The Section, files on specialists or specialist teams receive a one-word code name, printed across the file and restricted to very few people. When a solo or specialist team is employed on an operation, another designator word will refer to the operation and will be used for funding, reports, etc.

The Section's file name for Charlemagne is WEDGE. Thus CETUS WEDGE (second book of the Charlemagne Files) means an operation dubbed CETUS using the team called WEDGE.

Specialist

A team or solo operative used by Western governments for black operations conducted without fingerprints in high-risk situations expected to involve death.

GLOSSARY OF USEFUL TERMS (GUT)

AC - Aircraft Commander. The pilot who flies from the left seat of the cockpit and is in command of the aircraft, its crew, and any passengers.

AGE - Aircraft Ground Equipment. Air Force term for what is sometimes called ground support equipment in civilian contexts. Includes things like ground power units, air start units, dollies, jacks, lights, tugs, and tractors.

AFSC - Air Force Specialty Code, also called a career field in casual conversation. Designated by an alpha-numeric code that identifies a person's specific job and skill level.

Babysitter - term devised by the author to indicate those who provide logistic cover and support to the more dangerous operatives.

Bear - NATO name for the Russian TU-95, a strategic bomber used by the Soviets for reconnaissance missions at or over the boundaries of US airspace. Fighters, especially those from Alaskan or coastal bases, intercepted these forays regularly, a mutual game played by US reconnaissance platforms and MIG fighters near Soviet airspace.

Bring-Up Investigation: An expansion of a security investigation to add information because of a time-lapse, usually five years, since the last investigation, or to require additional details for a higher level of clearance.

Class B's - (Air Force) Blue uniform with shirt and tie but not the more formal blue coat.

Class B bachelor - person on temporary duty away from his/her home unit who removes his or her wedding ring for reasons not having to do with safety around the aircraft.

Cockroaches in the car - Okinawa's climate is hot and quite humid. Americans stationed there often buy their cars very used, somewhat rusty, and if not already home to the local insect wildlife, eventually infested. It is advisable at night to shoo them off the seat before sitting down.

COMSEC - Communications Security.

HUMINT - Human Intelligence. Not a comment on the thinking power of Homo sapiens. This refers to the gathering of information and leverage through the use of human relations, manipulations, and interactions.

Kadena Air Base - Large U.S. Air Force base on Okinawa, Japan. Known as the Keystone of the Pacific, it is home to the 18th Wing. Twenty thousand military members and federal employees and their dependents live or work on the base.

Making regular - Only graduates of the Air Force Academy are commissioned as regular officers when they become second lieutenants. All others, such as ROTC and OTS graduates, are commissioned as reserve officers even though they are on full-time active duty. Approximately four years later, a promotion board decides whether such officers should be offered regular commissions, usually when they pin on captain. It is the first real mark of successful career progression for a non-academy grad, though nothing tangible goes with it. One's boss knows one made it, and that means everything.

MREs - meals, ready to eat. Modern successors to K-rations and other attempts at field rations.

O-6 - A full colonel, as opposed to a lieutenant colonel. Also popularly referred to as a full bird colonel, because of the eagle insignia of rank.

Okuma Military Resort, Okinawa - Beach resort on Okinawa for use by armed forces personnel, federal employees, and their dependents.

Q - colloquial term for the BOQ or VOQ, bachelor officer quarters (for permanent duty) or visiting officer quarters (for those on temporary duty).

Škorpion - Czech-made submachine pistol.

Skoshi KOOM - Iconic restaurant on Kadena Air Base, now called Jack's Place after the man who made it the favorite haunt of so many, including the author. Skoshi is Japanese for small and KOOM stands for Kadena Officers' Open Mess.

Squadron Officer School - a military education course for company-grade officers (lieutenants and captains) held at Maxwell AFB, Montgomery, AL. At the time of Captain Nolan's attendance, it would have been 12 weeks long. Selection for in-residence attendance was somewhat competitive.

Tanker - An aircraft that refuels other airplanes in flight. A tanker of the 909th Air Refueling Squadron is a Boeing 707 designated as the KC-135. At the time of this story, the crew of a 135 included the aircraft commander, co-pilot, navigator, and boom operator.

TDY - Temporary duty, usually requiring travel away from one's permanent duty station.

UCMJ - Uniform Code of Military Justice - legal foundation of military conduct. All military members are subject to its jurisdiction, regardless of their location.

Zoomie - Graduate of the United States Air Force Academy

GLOSSARY OF GAME NAMES

Frank Cardova: long-time babysitter of Charlemagne; later, head of The Section; his real name is Leo Vilseck; Section nickname is Buddy.

Jay Turner: FBI counterintelligence agent with a private agenda; no aliases.

Mack: so dubbed by Western babysitters because he uses a knife at times; leader and decision maker of Charlemagne; called Misha by other members of his team; probable real name is Michael; last name is unknown.

The Frenchman: marksman and technical expert of Charlemagne; real name is Louis; last name unknown.

Vasily Sobieski: deceased explosives expert and martial artist whose father was a noted solo specialist; no aliases.

Charlie Taylor: marksman; son of Mack; probable real name is Michael; last name unknown.

Steve Donovan: recent new member of Charlemagne; martial artist; former fighter pilot; abandoned real name was Daniel Martin Kessler.